Be h **Behn, Harry**
    The faraway lurs

Date Due   66—63

APR 11 69 9			

The God of the spring claims Heather for
his own when she falls in love with a warrior
of Sun People.

7-9

THE FARAWAY LURS

CHILDREN'S BOOKS

Roderick
Windy Morning
All Kinds of Time
The Two Uncles of Pablo
The Wizard in the Well
The Painted Cave
The Little Hill
(*all published by Harcourt, Brace & World*)

The House Beyond the Meadow (*Pantheon Books*)
Timmy's Search (*The Seabury Press*)

POETRY

Siesta (*Golden Bough Press*)
Sombra (*Christtreu*, Copenhagen)
Rilke's Duino Elegies, translation (*Peter Pauper Press*)
Haiku Harvest, translation (*Peter Pauper Press*)

The Faraway Lurs

HARRY BEHN

THE WORLD PUBLISHING COMPANY

CLEVELAND AND NEW YORK

*The drawings for chapter heads
were designed by the author*

Published by The World Publishing Company
2231 West 110th Street, Cleveland 2, Ohio
Published simultaneously in Canada by
Nelson, Foster & Scott Ltd.
Library of Congress Catalog Card Number: 63-9658

3WP1264

TO

CHRISTINA LAWRENCE DODGE

THIS *is not the story I intended to tell. I had meant to write about Maren Christensen who was born on a farm in Denmark almost a hundred years ago.*

Before I knew her she had come to America, had learned English, and was a young woman of fashion in early-day San Francisco, where she also sold life insurance soon after that business was invented.

She was twenty-three.

On the Fourth of July, 1881, driving her own tandem team with matching coach dogs, she went as a guest of the Governor of California out to the gold fields to see a gold mine. There, her guide was a young miner who had also come from Denmark. He had bought a mine in Colorado, but found that two other men had already bought the same mine, and so he was about to go prospecting in Arizona Territory.

When the Governor's party left the gold fields, Maren locked one of her coach dogs in a tool shed. What she

9

hoped would happen, did. The young miner returned the dog to her in San Francisco, and she became an Arizona pioneer.

By the time I was aware that I was her son, she had already become a personage in Prescott, a small mining town in Arizona, the Territory's first capital.

When I was a little boy, she told me about her own happy childhood on a beautiful farm called Ballesgaard, near the village of Egtved in Denmark, where she had lived until she was eighteen. When I was grown, and she was gone, all I could remember of what she had told me was an idyllic mood. And so I went to Egtved to find out what influences could have produced such a joyous, gentle, and spirited person.

The story I thought I was looking for turned out to be something I hadn't expected. It was about another girl who lived in the same part of Denmark three thousand years ago.

I don't know the real name of this prehistoric girl. I have called her Heather Goodshade because her village lay between low sandy hills covered with heather and a great oak forest deep with shade.

I don't know what Egtved was called in Heather's time. Three hundred years ago it was Egetrae, seven hundred years ago, Ekthyuf, and before that, Ejte— all of these strange names meaning the Oak Tree. This suggested that long ago when people worshiped trees a sacred tree had grown there. Three thousand years ago the beech trees fighting for sunlight had not yet crowded out the older forests of oak. The climate was milder and sunnier than it is today.

One of the first things I wanted to see in Egtved was a mound of earth as big as a barn where my mother used to go on summer mornings to look out over the valley and listen to skylarks singing. The younger children believed a dragon once lived under this mound. The old people said it was where trolls still had their den. The Lutheran priest, who was also schoolmaster in those days, thought it was the grave of a viking. It was not far from where old Gorm was buried, at Jelling, where his son, Harold Bluetooth, had become the first Christian king of Denmark about a thousand years ago. That is what my mother believed, that the mound was the tomb of a viking.

From Ballesgaard I walked across the fields to see this ancient mound. What I found was a shallow pit half filled with a few damp rocks. The present schoolmaster told me what had happened.

In the spring of 1921, Peter Platz was plowing his pasture, scraping a little more flat land off the edges of the mound as he had been doing for years. He knew it was a grave, and was not surprised when his plowshare struck an oak log, a primitive coffin.

Some farmers might have looted it of treasure, since

gold and silver were often found in viking tombs. But Mr. Platz knew that if he robbed it, the story of who was buried there would be lost forever. And so he did the right thing. He telephoned the Royal Museum in Copenhagen and reported what he had found.

Professor Thomas Thomsen replied a little wearily that he would come to Egtved to investigate. From what Mr. Platz told him he knew it was not a viking burial, but much older. He had already opened many graves of this kind. Several of them were on display in cases in the museum, with their skeletons and objects of bronze. There was a sameness to all of them. But one thing Farmer Platz had said made Professor Thomsen wonder if this grave might not be a little different.

It was. It was a wet grave. It was not quite like any ever found before. The ancient people seemed to have an old understanding of the earth. They wanted the important person buried there to last for a long time. And so the coffin carved out of an oak log was placed on a platform of stones and covered in such a way that seepage from a small spring would keep it cool and damp.

When the coffin was opened in the museum, there was no skeleton. No bones at all. Acid from the damp wood had dissolved them away. What Professor Thomsen saw when he carefully unfolded a cowhide, then a woolen blanket, was a girl who had lived thousands of years ago. She was about eighteen years old.

Tannic acid from the oak had preserved her hair, her woolen blouse and short fringed skirt, her fingernails, and her skin. She was pressed a little flat, but her face and her body were visible enough to show that she had been beautiful.

After a few moments, the delicate outline of her skin dried out and she faded away, leaving only her blonde hair tied in a pony tail, her charming little costume, and ten neatly manicured fingernails.

Here was a mysterious and exciting discovery.

And the things buried with her were mysterious. This was a grave from the early Bronze Age when a person important enough to be so carefully buried, either a man or a woman, would be wearing fine jewelry, usually a pair of matched bracelets. But here were two quite different from each other, and not at all well made. Also, where her head had lain was a tiny bronze earring—such a worthless little trinket, it makes us wonder why she wore it.

Perhaps she wasn't a Bronze Age girl at all, but a Stone Age girl. The two ways of life went on side by side for many years. Some tribes still lived in the forest as they had for hundreds of years, still cutting trees with flint axes, still gathering wild fruit and nuts and seeds, farming a little, still hunting with bows and stone-pointed arrows. From time to time other tribes wandered by, herding cattle, hunting or fighting with bronze swords and axes. But stone axes cut trees quite well, and the simple forest people had no use for swords since they never fought wars. When enemies came by, they simply disappeared among the trees. Perhaps this girl was a forest girl.

The most impressive of her treasures was a bronze sun-disk she wore on her belt. It was about six inches across, carved with spirals and circles. Like her bracelets, the workmanship was not the best. A beginner in the craft might have made it. Perhaps a boy from some wandering tribe.

A small bark box with skeins of thread in it proved that she was practical and could sew. She might even have woven her own dress. But she must have had someone to polish her nails and comb her hair. Her comb was there. And a package of bones that had not dissolved away because they had been hardened by burning. They were the bones of a little girl about ten years old. She might have been a slave.

There was also a flower of milfoil and a frond of fern. And a small bark bucket which chemists found had had in it a pleasant drink made from marsh myrtle, cranberries, and honey. These tell us she was buried in summer, probably a hot summer when a person would be thirsty on her travels to another world.

After reading Professor Thomsen's report and a few other books on Danish archaeology, I decided that the

Oakwood Girl must have been the daughter of the chief of a tribe who lived in the forest, used stone tools and worshiped trees, and that her bronze jewelery had been given to her by a boy of some wandering tribe who worshiped the sun.

Today, a statue of her stands near the village of Egtved. The artist has seen her as I do in imagination—beautiful, gentle, curious about life, happily alive, and in love.

When you read her story, you may be surprised to find those ancient people so much like people today. Some as gentle, some as savage. It seems a very long time ago when the Achaeans had just come out of the north to Greece to start what we call western civilization. Three thousand years ago. But three thousand years is only about a hundred lifetimes. From father to son to son and so on, a hundred lifetimes is only a hundred people. You can't imagine the billions of your ancestors even a few hundred years ago, but you can imagine every person in one direct line from Heather's time. They wouldn't fill all the seats in a modern transport plane.

It is surprising we have come so far. But it is more surprising we haven't come farther when you think of what had been done and thought in Heather's time; even as long before that time as from then to now, when her Aryan ancestors had already composed wonderful poems—which you may still read. Even twenty thou-

sand years ago, when ice still covered most of Europe, her cave-dwelling ancestors had painted wonderful pictures—which you may still see.

And so it seems that whatever makes us what we are—customs, traditions, and heritage—are much older than we realize.

Until long after Heather's time there was no writing in Denmark. Only the suggestions of her beauty, and the few remains of what someone thought she might want with her in another world, tell the story. If what I have imagined doesn't seem quite the way things were, you must remember in your own dreams what did happen, and that story will be just as true.

Harry Behn

THE FARAWAY LURS

THE SUMMER DAYS were long. Twilight had hardly begun when it was dawn and up rose the sun again, hot above the sandy, heather-covered hills. But deep in the forest, east a little way to the sea and far to the north, all was shadowy and cool, and still, with a stillness stirred only by the ticking of an insect, the whirring of a wing.

In this green stillness, a slender girl walked round the trunk of a tremendous tree, looking up into its branches. Her dove-blonde hair was tied behind her head with a green cord. Her eyes were blue, her skin delicately fair, her blouse and short fringed skirt moss green. She was barefoot.

The tree Heather was planning to climb was old and mossy. Its leaves spread so densely above her that only a few rays of sunlight sifted through them, like flickering webs of flame. When they rustled in a wind their voice was only the peaceful voice of a tree. No one could mistake their whispering for words. The earth below was not trampled by the feet of dancing worshipers but covered with a tufted carpet of moss and ferns. This tree was not a god. It was only one of thousands of oaks in the forest, a little taller than most, with one great branch curving out from its trunk, then upward, spreading back through smaller branches on the other side. It was an easy tree to climb.

When Heather had decided how to go from one branch to the next, she took a birch-bark bucket from the slave girl who stood beside her and tied it to the fringe of her belt. Then, easily as a cat, she climbed into the tree and was soon lost among its leaves.

The little slave tried not to be afraid for Heather, but she was. Trees still frightened her. Until three summers ago she had lived in a tent on a grassy plain where the wind sang and the sun burned distant mountains to a blue haze. She wished the Forest People lived in such an open place. But still she was glad she had been captured by Goodshade, who was Heather's father.

When she was first captured, she was as wild as a small frightened animal. She would not speak. She would only buzz through her teeth. That is why she was called Buzz. But Heather had tamed her with kindness until she was more like a little sister than a slave.

Sometimes, though, you could still see the wildness in her brown eyes, when someone teased her or mentioned the gods. She did not like the gods, any of them.

As Heather climbed high into the tree she was thinking only of the good taste of honey mixed with crushed marsh-myrtle leaves and cranberries and water from the spring. Honey was the hardest to find. She had followed bees homing toward this tree and had found their hive high in a dead branch as white as bone. When she climbed out toward this branch, bees began to dart at her, to circle angrily about her, and she called down to Buzz, "Quiet them!"

Under the tree the child began to hum, and the bees that had been storming about Heather flew back to their hive.

No one could explain why this happened, not even Buzz. Her grandmother had taught her how to speak to bees to quiet them. But she would never speak to them for anyone except Heather. Blue Wing had tried to hum the same sound, but it seemed only to make the bees more angry. None of the other girls ever tried to rob a hive. They were afraid of bees, even of one bee gathering honey from a wildflower. After the girls were ten they seldom climbed trees, and never the big oaks in the forest. They were afraid of being teased by the boys. No one ever teased Heather about climbing, because she could climb better than any of them.

Now, as she balanced herself on a slim branch above the hollow white bough, she reached through a humming swarm of bees into the hive. She crushed the comb and scooped its sweet treasure into her bucket. Not one bee stung her, because Buzz was speaking to them from below.

When her bucket was full, Heather calmly and gently brushed the clinging swarm off her arms and licked the sticky honey off her fingers. Suddenly she was stung. "Quiet them!" she called to Buzz.

The child below was silent.

Again Heather was stung, on both arms, and again she called, a little angrily, "Why do you stop buzzing and let me be stung!"

"Because I heard a sound I don't like," said Buzz.

Heather listened. Bees still hummed about her, but she did not notice them. She had heard the sound that frightened Buzz. From the south came a soft, dark, mysterious hooting.

Almost at the edge of the world a cloud of dust arose twisting in a wind. Under this cloud Heather saw wagons, like beetles, and men, as small as ants, men riding horses, marching, driving before them a herd of cattle, people and cattle and horses moving toward a small brown lake ringed by a margin of trees and grass. Then, out of the dust, glinting in the sun, a strange object appeared. It stood upright, tall as a tree, on a chariot drawn by six white horses. As the chariot turned, she saw that it had six wheels, and the object on it was a great golden disk that sent out flashes of light as bright as the sun itself, like arrows, into her eyes.

Heather had heard about this golden disk of the Sun People. She had heard about their bronze axes and swords and their strange wild ways. She had heard about them from her father and from Buzz.

Buzz did not like the Sun People. Only three years ago, when she was seven, they had thrown her into a swamp as a sacrifice. Chief Goodshade had found her sinking into dirty, black, smelly mud. He had killed the sun-priest and saved her, and given her to his daughter as a birthday present. Three small blue dots above Buzz's eyebrows were the marks of the Sun People.

Heather remembered a story her father had told about one tribe of Sun People who had marched up from the south seeking grass and water for their cattle. It had been a very hot summer, like this one. The brown lake in the middle of the heath was dry, and all the grass around it had dried up. But the spring of Oakwood still splashed out its pure cool water. The thirsty Sun People did not know this spring was sacred. There had been a battle between long bronze swords and stone-tipped arrows. But soon so many forest archers appeared silently, from villages no one knew were there, that the Sun People began to wonder why they were fighting and marched away. They marched away to the north, ate their cattle, and became hunters of wolves and deer. They trapped fish in the sea and gathered amber along the shore. With their bronze axes they cut trees and built ships, and sailed them all over the world, trading amber and hides for bronze and gold. This had all happened before Heather was born. They still lived up there somewhere and were said to have become fat and tame. They never again bothered the village of Oakwood.

As Heather listened to the dark, distant hooting she could see now what made the sound. The sun-chariot had stopped near the lake. A cloud of dust, slowly settling, hid everything for a moment. Then, out of the glittering cloud, two men marched into the meadows, blowing trumpets that curled up over their heads as tall again as themselves.

Heather had heard about these bronze trumpets. They were called lurs, and were used by the sun-priests to speak to the sun, to tame it, as Buzz spoke to bees to tame them. Behind these hooting trumpets came the chariot with its shining disk, and after that, horses and cattle, and after those, the Sun People, a whole tribe of them.

They seemed to be dancing, clustering together, spreading out, coming together again, moving slowly over the green grass by the lake into the country of the Forest People.

Heather could not brush the sound of the lurs out of her mind. It clung as the bees had clung to her arms when she reached into their hive to rob them.

To her, all faraway sounds had always seemed like dreams—the lowing of a cow at dusk, the barking of a dog on a frosty night, the chopping of a flint ax deep in the forest, children playing in a meadow—these were all dreams full of memories. But what the dream might mean behind the dark sound of the lurs she could not quite remember. It was the most dangerous and exciting sound she had ever heard, as if its sweetness might sting her at any moment as the bees had stung her.

She knew she should be afraid of this enchantment, and she was. But her fear was exciting and only made her want to be close among the wild Sun People as they blew their trumpets and clashed their swords and chanted and danced before their golden sun-disk.

Heather had been so absorbed in this waking dream that she hardly remembered climbing down the tree, and was surprised to find herself out of the dense wood and almost home.

Walking beside a bramble hedge that enclosed a small field, she heard her father singing to himself. She stood on tiptoe to peek over the hedge and saw him chopping weeds among the wheat. She ran on toward the zigzag gate through the briars. There, she paused and held her breath, listening to the peaceful sounds of the village. No one seemed to know of the danger that threatened them, her father, or anyone. In all her eighteen years she had never before known real danger to come so close. She shivered as she imagined savage warriors rushing down on her village and destroying it!

As she stood there, Blue Wing came out of the forest dragging a heavy oak log by one end. When he saw her, he dropped the log and sat on it and wiped the sweat from his face. Heather ran quickly toward him to tell him what she had seen—the Sun People putting up a whole village of tents around the brown lake!

She was so excited she could hardly remember what

she had seen and what she imagined. It might be better, she thought, to tell it even badly to Blue Wing and let him tell it more soberly to her father.

Heather knew that everyone expected her someday to marry Blue Wing, which seemed a pleasant idea when he smiled at her or when he made up a song for her, even the kind one sang to children. But when he scolded her for climbing trees or getting honey all over her and dirt on top of the honey, and told her to go and wash her face and grow up, then she thought it would be nicer to marry anyone else at all; then she noticed that Blue Wing was shaped like a bear and had a snub nose.

But whatever Heather thought of him when he treated her like a child, she really liked him very much, and was proud of him, and glad that everyone else liked him. Most of the time she supposed that someday she would marry him. He had never said anything about this to her. But she knew what was in his mind. And so did little Buzz, who had heard him talking to Goodshade. Buzz had heard them agree that Blue Wing would ask for Heather on the night of the next full moon.

Everyone knew what would happen then. Chief Goodshade would pretend to be angry and drive Blue Wing away. But when the moon came up, there would be a slow procession down to the sacred oak tree. Heather would be dressed in a beautiful robe of soft white doe skins her mother had made for her. Around the tree until dawn there would be dancing and singing and sacrifices of sheep and a great feast. As the sun arose, Blue Wing would return dressed in the hide of a red deer with the antlers fastened on his head. He would dance proudly and while everyone carefully pretended not to see him he would steal Heather and take her to a new house he had built for her. She knew why a few days ago he had shot a red deer, and why he was now cutting timbers and shaping them. It was what everyone expected.

But even when Blue Wing smiled he was still not the tall, handsome young man who often stood watching her just beyond the edge of her dreams. She had never spoken of this shadowy person even to Buzz, or spoken to him; and he had never spoken to her. She did not expect ever to meet him in this world. But she did wish that Blue Wing was not shaped so much like a bear and that his nose was not quite so snubbed.

These were her thoughts as she ran to tell him about the Sun People.

He sat on the oak log and smiled pleasantly, watching her, not listening to a word she said except that she had climbed the tall curved tree. "Don't you know that's the most dangerous tree in the forest," he said severely. "It's too high for a girl to climb, and it's full of dead branches. Anyway, you shouldn't be climbing trees any more." Even though he looked at her almost as if she were grown-up, what he said was what one would say to a child, and it made her angry.

"All right then, I won't tell you what I discovered when I was up there!"

"I can guess. A beehive. But all the honey you carried away seems to be on your face and in your hair."

This reminded Heather that she had left her bucket of honey hanging in the tree while she was listening to the lurs just before she swung on a limber branch down to the ground. "I forgot the honey," she said. "And if you had any manners, you'd listen to *why* I forgot it!"

Blue Wing laughed, and stood up. Holding her arms, he kissed her sticky, grimy cheek.

She turned away from him sulkily and said, "Why don't you tell me to go and wash my face, the way you usually do!"

He was serious, and a little sad. "I don't always. Sometimes you're so beautiful I hardly dare to look at you." Picking up the end of the oak beam, he began to drag it away toward the meadow beyond the village.

Heather ran after him and stepped in front of him. He stopped, but still held the end of the heavy timber, looking at her.

"Please," she said, "let me tell you what I heard and saw when I was up in the tree!"

"I'll try to listen," he said patiently.

"I heard lurs! For the first time I heard the lurs of

the Sun People. I saw their sun-chariot, and men riding horses and driving herds of cattle. I saw more people than I have ever seen before in my whole life putting up tents down by the brown lake!"

Blue Wing watched her for a moment. Then he let the end of the timber drop to the ground. "Have you told this to your father?"

She shook her head.

He walked toward the field, and she followed him. They went through the zigzag gate in the hedge, up to Goodshade, and Heather told her father what she had seen.

The chief's strong lean face and blue eyes remained perfectly calm. When she had told everything she could remember, he said, "These are not the first Sun People to pass this way. A long time ago we taught them that horsemen and swords are helpless among trees, and that our archers fight invisibly. There is still plenty of water in the brown lake and grass around it. I think this tribe will not bother us." He picked up his hoe made of an elk's antler and began to chop weeds among the wheat.

Heather and Blue Wing went silently away through the bramble hedge, across the meadow, and up the slope of a mound as big as a small hill with five great boulders on top. It was the mound of an ancient grave. They climbed up on the boulders and looked toward the south.

They couldn't quite see beyond the sandy hills, but a haze of dust and smoke from campfires hung in the air.

"My father doesn't seem to be afraid of the Sun People," she said. "Are you?"

"A little," he admitted.

"Suppose they've learned to fight among trees, not on horses or with swords, but the way we do, with bows and arrows?"

"I was wondering the same thing," said Blue Wing. He sat beside her on the capstone of the mound.

"What would you do," she asked, "if you were my father?"

"I'd send someone down there to find out if they *have* learned to use bows and arrows."

"That's what I'd do," she said eagerly. "Why don't we go there, you and I, and find out!"

He glanced at her. Her face was flushed with excitement.

"I mean," she added, "tonight, when it's dark."

He shook his head and laughed. "I don't understand you, Heather. You're supposed to be a girl."

"And you are supposed to be a man!" she said hotly. "You almost are, anyway. But you're more afraid than I am."

"I don't think you're afraid at all. Only curious."

"Of course, I am," she said.

"Well, forget about going over there. You could be

captured and made a slave, or be sacrificed to their sun-god."

Heather glanced at him slyly. "Buzz would go with me."

"Oh, no, she wouldn't," said Blue Wing. "She knows how dangerous they are."

Heather had seen a shadow moving along the grass below the stones and guessed who it was. She leaned over, and there in the shade sat little Buzz with her arms clasped about her knees, pretending to be invisible.

When the child saw Heather smiling down at her, she frowned. "I heard everything you and Blue Wing said. Your father knew days ago those people were coming this way. Last night he sent Littleman out to Birdsong Village to tell the people on that side of the heath to get ready for war."

Blue Wing flushed. "How do you know?"

"Oh, I hear things," said Buzz. "Other men have gone to warn the villages on this side."

Blue Wing was unhappy. "I wonder why Goodshade didn't send me. Or tell me what was happening."

Heather patted his cheek. "He will when you're a little more grown-up." She jumped down beside Buzz.

Above them, Blue Wing's good-natured laugh rang out, and he pounced down beside them. He looked at Heather. "From now on I won't say a thing, no matter what you do." He looked at Heather until she turned away. At that moment she liked him more than she ever had before.

He said, "It doesn't matter if they have archers or not. We'll be ready for them!" He loped away down the mound. It was strange how much like a bear he seemed, a strong, gentle, friendly bear. He wasn't very handsome, but no one was so clever at making arrow points.

Buzz lay back on the grass, walking her feet up the side of the stone. "Do you love Blue Wing?" she asked.

Heather was gazing dreamily at the smoke and dust above the camp of the Sun People. "I don't know," she said.

Buzz walked her feet down the stone and sat up. "Until you heard the lurs, you did." She made a motion with her fingers like a bee flying and buzzed. "You've let those bad people tame you before you've even seen them!"

"I have not!"

"Then why do you want to go to their camp?"

"Because I'm curious, that's all."

"No!" said Buzz angrily. "Because they've put a spell on you with their lurs, that's why!" With quick little steps she floated away down the mound.

Heather sighed and slowly followed her toward the village.

Early the next morning Heather bathed in the pool below the spring, and Buzz combed her hair and tied it back with a green cord and put a sprig of fern and milfoil in it, and a rose with five loose red petals and a golden center. Then they went through the woods to the twisted tree to get the honey Heather had left there.

A bird whistled among the leaves. The spring splashed in the stillness. It was such a clear, quiet, golden morning it was hard to think the Sun People could be very dangerous. But Buzz remembered that it had been just this kind of a morning when the sun-priest had wakened her, and carried her away, and thrown her into a swamp.

While Heather climbed the tree Buzz sat on the moss and waited, trying to be patient. The bucket of honey hung on a snag only a little way up, but Heather climbed on past it until she was out of sight among the leaves.

Suddenly, the lurs sounded!

They were still sounding, far away in the stillness, when Buzz found herself running wildly through the forest. She sat down, still trembling, and dug up a few roots and ate them.

When the lurs stopped sounding, Heather came down from the high branches of the tree and tied the bucket of honey to her belt. She balanced herself on the big branch that swept out almost level with the ground, and called to Buzz. There was no answer. She caught a limber bough that swung down and set her bare feet gently on the ground.

She had not seen anyone move under the tree, but there, in the leafy light, a young man stood glaring at her, his bronze sword drawn halfway out of its sheath.

She was startled, but not afraid. The young man was slender and handsome. He stood with his feet planted firmly apart, trying to look like a fierce warrior. His brown tunic was not as well woven as her blouse. He wore shoes of painted leather with pointed toes. She had never worn shoes.

They stared curiously at each other. Then the boy frowned even more fiercely and asked, "What did you see up there?"

"Bees," said Heather. "They stung me when I robbed their honey. Would you like some?" She untied the bucket from her belt and held it out to him.

He snapped his sword back into its scabbard and stubbornly folded his arms across his chest. "I meant, what did you see out there?" He nodded toward the south.

Heather pretended not to hear him. She mixed a little honey with moss and blobbed it on her arms where the bees had stung her. "I don't blame them. It was their honey. They have every right to sting people who rob them."

The young warrior was annoyed. "Don't pretend you didn't see people out there, and cattle. You must have heard the lurs. I could hear them down here."

"I don't hear them now."

"You don't, because the ceremony is over."

"How long are those people going to stay down there?"

"I am one of those people," he said proudly. Then he answered her question. "Until our animals drink the lake dry and eat all the grass around it."

She looked at him thoughtfully. He was no longer trying to be fierce. He seemed a little embarrassed. She guessed he was younger than she had thought. A small bronze razor dangled from his belt, but his slender tanned face showed no sign that he had ever had to use it.

He glanced at her more pleasantly and asked, "Where do you live?"

"Not very far away."

He frowned. "I know that!"

"How do you know?"

"Because a girl like you wouldn't go far from her home, alone."

"I'm not alone."

He lifted his eyebrows and peered into the forest on every side. He saw no one. He listened and heard no unusual sound.

She smiled. "My father is the chief of a village quite close to here. He's very strong and brave, so if you *are* thinking about robbing us—"

"The way you robbed the bees? We just might, if you have anything we want!" He was acting like a warrior again. He drew his sword and held it out to her, hilt-first. "Look at that!"

She touched the hand-grip decorated with gold, and smiled again. "It's beautiful!"

"Feel how sharp the blade is!"

She took the sword. It was so heavy she had to hold it with both hands, and he laughed. "Watch this!" He took it from her by the blade, swung it once over his

head, and threw it toward the oak tree. It turned in the
air and with a solid thump stuck point-first in the trunk.
He tightened his belt and started toward the tree with
a little swagger. Then he turned back and said, "Any of
our warriors can do the same thing. Even the girls.
Their swords aren't as heavy though."

Her eyes opened wide in surprise. "Are the girls in
your tribe warriors too?"

"Certainly."

"Don't you have enough men?"

He laughed. "You saw how many men are out there.
Except for the slaves they're all warriors. The girls are,
too, because they like to fight. Anyway, they have to.
They aren't allowed to have a husband until they've
killed an enemy."

"I don't call that a very nice custom."

He hesitated and looked away. Then he said, "Neither
do I. I hate it. All they think about is racing their ponies
and acting wild. I used to like horses. Do you?"

"I've never seen one close."

"I used to ride all day long. With my father. Now I'd
rather walk. You can see things better. I used to like to
hunt, especially wild pigs, with a spear. Now my father
doesn't ride any more, and hunting doesn't interest
me."

"What does?"

"Making things." He came close to her and showed

her the bracelets on his arms, on each wrist and above his elbows. "I made these."

"And your sword, too?"

He nodded proudly. "My father taught me. He used to be the best swordsmith in the world. Now I am." He glanced at her, a little ashamed of his boasting, and said, "But I'm not as brave as you are. I'd be afraid to climb up where you were, even without bees stinging me."

"I'm not brave." She smiled. "I'd be afraid to ride a horse or to kill anybody, the way girls do in your tribe. I couldn't even hurt anybody."

"I don't like to, myself," he said.

He went over to the tree, pulled out his sword, and slipped it back in its scabbard. "What's your name?" he asked.

"Heather."

"Mine's Wolf Stone. My father is Chief Great Elk. I'm his youngest son. He has twenty-five sons. Maybe more. Most of them are warriors. Oxenstar is next youngest to me, and he's already a captain. All of our important families have animal names. Except our sun-priests, like Troll Tamer. I like your name."

"It was my grandmother's. She had brown eyes, like yours."

"Maybe she came from one of our tribes."

"She did like to sit in the sun, especially when she was old."

"Did she have marks like this over her eyebrows?" He pointed to three small blue dots above his brows, like Buzz's.

Heather shook her head.

"Then she couldn't have been one of us. Just because she liked the sun doesn't prove anything. Everybody does."

"I don't."

He glanced at her, and then up at the flecks of light among the leaves. "You mustn't say things like that!"

"I meant, I don't like to be out in the bright sun very much. I get all red."

He shook his head as if she amused him. "I guess you Forest People don't know very much. I've heard you think some tree or other is a god, or some spring of water. Is that what you think?"

She nodded.

He reached up and touched the curved branch that swept away among the leaves. "Is this your god?"

"Oh, no!"

He smiled pleasantly. "Worshiping trees is pretty silly. But then, how would you know any better if no one ever taught you anything. Troll Tamer says you still make axes out of stone."

"We do. And arrow points for hunting. The prettiest ones are for offerings."

"Do you ever offer them to the sun?"

"I told you," said Heather, "we don't think the sun is very friendly."

He laughed. "That's the stupidest thing I ever heard! Don't you know you wouldn't be here, nothing would be in this world except for the sun? And where do you think people go when they die? Down under the ground?"

"We bury dead people under the ground."

"So do we. But do you think they stay there? Of course not. The sun takes them on his ship back to the land we all come from. A tree can't be a god. It dies just like people. You think about it."

"I am."

He smiled. "You're lucky I came along to teach you something." He dipped his hand into the bucket of honey and lay back on the moss, licking the sweet off his fingers. "Look at the color of honey or gold or amber— all the most sacred things are the color of the sun." He turned on his side and looked at her. "Your hair is almost sun color."

She was embarrassed. And so was he. He lay there looking up into the tree. "The first thing my father made out of bronze was a sun-disk. My mother always wore it. Someday it will be mine . . . to give to anyone I want to give it to."

In the drowsy stillness Heather heard a sound Wolf Stone didn't notice. She knew it was Buzz watching from somewhere, and called to her.

Wolf Stone leaped up, his hand on his sword hilt.

Heather laughed. "I told you I wasn't alone. My slave is out there somewhere. She used to be one of your people." Again Heather called. With quick small steps, Buzz came to her and took her hand. The little girl looked up at the stern face of the young warrior and began to buzz.

"Why is she making that sound at me?" he asked.

"She's afraid of you."

"Of me? I'm one of her own people. Those dots on her forehead prove it." He moved toward the child, who edged away from him and hid behind Heather. "Why is she afraid of me?"

"Because your sun-god tried to swallow her into a muddy marsh. My father saved her and gave her to me."

He took a deep breath and growled. "I suppose it's too much for your simple mind to understand that all gods have to be cruel. If they weren't, people would forget they have to die sometime. I suppose you believe everything in the world is peaceful and dreamy and half asleep. Like this gloomy green forest!" He looked about him and shuddered.

Heather said quietly, "I'd be ashamed of a god who has to prove how important he is by killing children."

Wolf Stone glared at her. Then he turned and walked haughtily away out of the forest.

"You see!" Buzz giggled. "He's like all the rest of them! Anyway, you told him what you think of his old sun-god!"

Heather had forgotten her bucket of honey again. Buzz picked it up and they walked back toward the village.

The child glanced up at Heather's dreaming face. "Don't you ever trust any of them!" she said. "In a few days their horses and cows will drink all the water in the brown lake. Then they'll come here and drink our spring dry and we'll all turn to dust and be blown away!"

"I don't think so," said Heather. "They will march away and not even come near our spring. They will go on to the north where they will eat their cattle and become hunters of wolves. They will gather amber and build ships and become fat and tame. Then we will forget them forever—all of them!"

"How do you know?" asked Buzz.

Heather sighed. "I don't. But that's how it *might* happen."

She was sorry she had made the young warrior angry.

THAT EVENING when the sun touched the tops of the trees and slanted long blue shadows across the meadow, Heather went out to the mound. Beyond the houses children were chanting and dancing in a game, an evening cricket was chirping, and cows in their bramble-hedged pasture were calling to be milked. She walked slowly up the mound toward the great stones looming against the blue sky. Above them a skylark fluttered and poured out its sweet twittering song; a rabbit scuttled into the little cave under the stones. She climbed up and sat on the capstone, and looked out over the vil-

45

lage and the fields and the forest she had known all her life. Until today she had thought that nothing of this would ever change. Now, in the shadows of evening, everything seemed more precious to her because tomorrow it might all be destroyed, overrun by shouting strangers, wild girls flashing swords, sun-priests setting fire to the cottages, cattle milling everywhere, trampling the pool below the spring, drinking it dry!

She had said nothing to her father and mother about meeting the young warrior of the Sun People. Buzz had said nothing. But Heather could not forget him.

Soon the round red sun burned down behind the tree that was her god. Beams of its light reached into the forest, glowing on the trunks, deepening the shadows. Then everything turned gray. The sun was gone. But the sacred tree was still there. And the spring was still there talking in the twilight.

Perhaps, thought Heather, there are three gods. Perhaps the sun is one of them, as Wolf Stone believes. But she could imagine nothing about such a god to love— not as she loved the tree for its quiet wisdom, or the spring for its happiness. Still, there was something about the sun that was strong and beautiful and dangerous. Like Wolf Stone. She sighed. She would never see him again. At least, not as a friend.

Forest People were usually quick to notice any sound or movement in their world of leaves. But Heather did not notice a shadow that moved through the dusk silently up the grassy slope of the mound. Her heart almost stopped as she looked down into the face of Wolf Stone.

"You see why I like to move on my own feet." He smiled. "Once I walked up to an antlered chieftain of deer and slapped him on the haunch. That's why my father sends me out scouting ahead."

Her heart was pounding so hard she could scarcely breathe.

He touched her bare foot with his fingers. "I'm sorry. I'm sorry I lost my temper."

She drew her foot away. "Why did you follow me?"

"To see where you lived." He looked down at the small straw-thatched timber houses scattered among the trees, at fires flickering under shelters where women were cooking. There was a good smell of crusty toasted wheat in the air. Children had stopped playing and were talking in low voices while they ate. Dogs had been fed and lay asleep about the fires. Cows had been milked and were munching grain. A lamb bleated sleepily.

Heather glanced at the boy as he gazed down at her village. She could almost hear him thinking, This is a peaceful village tonight. Tomorrow it will be ashes. Her eyes filled with tears. "You see how easy it would be to destroy us."

He smiled sadly. "That's why I followed you here. To tell you something."

It seemed a difficult thing for him to tell. He reached up and took her hand. "I want your village to stay the way it is." He spoke in a low voice. He was very serious. "I am the only one of my people who knows where this village is, here within the edge of the wood, with those low hills hiding it. I'm going to tell my father I found nothing here, that the village he is looking for is beyond, to the north, where other tribes of our people live. When he has gone that far I don't think he will come back."

Heather was puzzled. "Why is your father looking for this village?"

Wolf Stone was silent. He was gazing at the dark edge of the forest where one rounded oak tree rose above all the rest. "There is something your people must do," he said. "Tonight you must take your animals and dogs and children and women into the forest. You must stay there for a few days. Your warriors must not get excited and shout or try to follow us. They must not brag about how they scared Great Elk away. If he ever found out how I deceived him, he would come back here and kill every one of you!"

Heather held her breath. "If he finds out you lied to him, what will he do to you?"

"That is not important," said Wolf Stone stiffly.

She slid down the stone beside him. He stood like a warrior, looking out over her head.

"Would he kill you?"

He shrugged.

Trying to understand him, she asked, "Why does your father want to find this village?"

The boy turned away and spoke gruffly. "I told you we wanted only water and grass for our cattle and horses. That isn't true. There are lakes and meadows the whole length of this land. What Great Elk wants is wood. He wants to build a ship!"

"But there is wood everywhere!"

Wolf Stone glanced out at the tallest of all the trees in the forest. "There is only one tree he wants."

Heather's heart fluttered with fear.

"Everyone knows," he said, "that a ship built of wood from the tree of power can never be sunk. For two years my father has been searching for that tree. Someone has told him it grows in a village called Oakwood."

"Who told him?" she asked.

"Someone of your people."

"Who?"

Wolf Stone cried out impatiently, "I don't know! Possibly your slave girl who buzzed at me. She's one of us. Or was."

"It could never have been Buzz!" said Heather firmly.

"Whoever it was knows the tree and hates it and fears it and is a friend of our head sun-priest, Troll Tamer. That is all I know."

She moved away from him and asked angrily, "Why should I believe anything you say! Why should you care what happens to our tree or any of us!"

He took her hands gently and looked into her eyes as he said in a low voice, "Because you're not like any girl I've ever known." He released her hands and slipped away around the stones of the mound. When she ran to look for him he had vanished into the dusk.

NIGHT was not yet deep enough for stars to show. Blue Wing and Goodshade were sitting beside a small fire outside Littleman's house. They were shaping arrow shafts. The chief sighted along one, holding it toward the light of the fire.

Heather went quietly past them, unnoticed, on toward her house. Her eyes were full of silent tears. She was weeping because it was so kind and brave of Wolf Stone to risk his life for her!

Outside her door she brushed away her tears and tried to think how to tell her father what Wolf Stone had said to do—to take everyone into the forest for a few days until the Sun People had gone away. She wondered how to explain why the son of Great Elk would risk his life to save the village of Oakwood. Perhaps her mother would understand.

When she stepped into her house, Tree Woman was lighting a rush-light. This plump, gentle woman held up a lump of beeswax with a reed burning in it and looked into her daughter's face. There she saw wonder and a strange happiness and the stain of tears.

"Tell me," said her mother gently.

They sat down on an elk hide spread on the earth floor, and Heather told how the Sun People wanted to cut down their tree to build a ship.

"How did you learn this?" asked Tree Woman.

"From Wolf Stone, the son of Great Elk, who is their chief. Wolf Stone told me."

Her mother held her hand. "Have you fallen in love with this boy?"

"Oh, no!" said Heather quickly. "That would be terribly foolish. He's going away, tomorrow." Her lips trembled. "I'll never see him again, so how could I fall in love with him?"

Then she explained that her father must take everyone into the forest while Wolf Stone led the Sun People away. "So our village will not be noticed as they go by."

Her mother nodded. And Heather told how clever

Wolf Stone was, how strong and handsome and kind. What she did not tell was that someone in Oakwood was an enemy of the tree and wanted the Sun People to destroy it. She was afraid someone might think it was Buzz.

Tree Woman did not seem troubled by anything Heather told her. She simply said, "Before we speak to your father, perhaps we'd better ask those who see beyond to tell us what to do."

Together they went out under the first stars, past a pond where the sheep and cows drank, along a brook that trickled into it, on among reeds and rushes to a bathing pool, then up three stone steps to a brimming, rocky hollow into which water fell.

Heather kneeled to this talking spring and said in a whisper, "Make me as pure and clear as you are so I may speak the oldest words as happily as you do." Then she clung to her mother and wept.

Tree Woman washed away the tears from her face. The air was cool with water smells and warm with flower smells. The darkness stirred with small insect voices and the splashing of water.

"What does the spring say?" asked Heather softly.

Tree Woman listened. "She says you have been foolish to fall in love with a boy of the Sun People. She says that now she must laugh and weep forever."

Heather stood up and said angrily, "Then she had

better laugh and weep about everything in the world!"

"Perhaps so." Her mother smiled.

Heather walked down the stone steps to the path beside the stream. "I would like to hear what the tree says." Tree Woman followed her, shaking her head, chuckling and sighing.

It seemed a long way out to the tree. Suddenly, from under a darkness of leaves they stepped into a wide clearing under the open sky. In the center of this dusty bareness, under the stars, stood an oak tree so perfectly formed that it seemed only a tremendous mound of leaves. As they walked toward it the tree seemed to grow, to lift its under boughs free of the ground, higher and higher like wings, until a ceiling of leaves closed over them and they saw in the dimness before them the gray gnarled trunk that held up this living temple of a god.

They stood close to the trunk, unable to speak in the shadow and silence. When they began to see again, to hear the night sounds of the forest, Tree Woman said quietly, "He speaks."

"What does he say?" whispered Heather.

"He says the son of Great Elk is so new to the darkness of love that he has lost sight of what is true. He can never deceive his father."

Heather choked back a gasp of fear. "Then he will be killed!"

Tree Woman spoke again. "The tree asks us to wonder why Wolf Stone tells us to leave our homes."

"Because he loves me!" said Heather.

"If we hide in the forest, who will protect our tree from the sun-priests who hate him?"

"A god should know how to protect himself!"

Her mother listened again to the tree. A wind moved slowly through the leaves. "He tells us to stay in our homes."

"Then," said Heather bitterly, "there will be a war. Does he say there must be a war?"

Tree Woman listened.

The wind died away. The tree did not speak again.

THAT NIGHT Heather cried under her lambskin
covers until she was almost asleep. Then she was
wide awake again, angry at the tree for not trusting
Wolf Stone. She closed her eyes and was ashamed for
thinking such thoughts against that good and ancient
god. Far away in the forest a wolf howled, and she
thought it was the lurs leading an army of girl warriors
with swords to cut down the great peaceful tree. An owl
hooted and it seemed to be asking: Who told the Sun
People that the tree of power grows in Oakwood?

It could never have been Buzz! Buzz hated the Sun

People. She hated their god. She did not love any god. But she did love Heather, and would never do anything to hurt her.

Soon after midnight the stars faded from the sky, and it was dawn. The sun came up, and wings flashed as birds flew chirping among briars and bushes and over the swamp seeking their food.

Heather dressed and went outside. Everyone was still asleep. A golden silence lay over everything. The tree still towered above the forest. The spring still murmured pleasantly. Suddenly she could not believe that anything dreadful could possibly happen in such a beautiful world!

Buzz came outside, fastening her dress, happy to see Heather smiling.

Silent as deer they ran across the meadow and up the mound to its cap of stones.

Buzz found some nuts she had hidden in the little cave under the biggest boulder. She cracked the nuts, and they ate them for breakfast.

"All night I watched you sleeping," said Buzz.

Heather sighed. "I didn't sleep."

"Yes, you did! As if you had gone a long way away. Where were you? Can you remember? Was it a nice place?"

Heather shook her head. She couldn't remember sleeping at all.

Buzz sprawled on the grass and rolled like a puppy. Then she sat up and frowned. "Were you with *him?*"

"I can't remember."

And then she did. She remembered her dream! Wolf Stone was Chief of the Sun People. He told them to march into a swamp where they all sank and disappeared. Sadly, he stood watching her beyond the edge of her dream. Then, sadly he followed his people down into darkness forever.

Anything that might happen could never be so dreadful as this dream!

"If they want our tree," she sighed, "I think we should give it to them."

Buzz was surprised. "To the Sun People?"

Heather nodded.

"Why do they want it?"

"To make a ship."

The child thought for a moment. Then she clapped her hands happily. "A ship to sail away in! Then we'd be rid of them!"

Heather laughed, and her dream melted away. Still, half seriously, she thought that if the tree would give himself to the Sun People, Great Elk and Goodshade could be friends, and there would be no war. A god should be pleased to make everyone so happy. How much better to become a ship and move about all over the world than stubbornly to stay a tree and cause a war!

The bee stings on her arms began to itch, and she said to Buzz, "Get me something from the Swampwife to stop these bee stings from itching!"

Buzz, who was rolling on the grass, stood up and said firmly, "No!"

"It was your fault they stung me."

"The old woman won't be awake this early. Or if she is, she won't be back from eating toads down in the swamp."

"She does not eat toads!"

"I've seen her!"

"If she does, poor thing," said Heather, "it's only because she has nothing else to eat."

Buzz sputtered with disgust. "Poor thing! She's not poor. She has more than any of us. Amber as big as hawk's eggs, and a golden horn with pictures on it, and bronze pins and piles of bracelets!"

Heather was amazed. "The Swampwife has these things?"

Buzz nodded. "She keeps them in a hole under the firestone in her dirty little hut a goat wouldn't live in."

"Are you sure?"

"I saw them! I touched them!"

"How would you dare to go into her house! She might have come back and caught you."

"She was there all the time. She was outside on the ground, with her eyes open, where she fell down thump when I buzzed at her. If I hadn't buzzed, she would have pushed me into the swamp. How was I to know that patch of weeds was her garden! They stung my feet, so I pulled most of them up before she came out and yelled at me. When she fell down, I thought she was dead. She was stiff as wood, but she wasn't dead. She saw me go inside her house. When I came out again, her eyes were awake. Like a toad's eyes. She was making noises like a toad. If you want something to stop your itches, go and get it yourself!"

If what Buzz said was true, the person who hated the tree, who had told the Sun People about it, was the Swampwife! How else would she have amber and gold and bronze? Those were things only the Sun People were rich enough to own.

Heather walked down the mound toward a grove of birch trees. Buzz followed her and ran in front of her. "Please don't go there," she begged.

No one knew very much about the old Swampwife. The only time anyone saw her was when they went to her for magic herbs, which always seemed to cure any sickness. But no one liked her. When you gave her a piece of meat or fruit to pay her, you could never tell what she would do. Sometimes she would snatch the food and spit on it, or throw it down and stamp on it. But sometimes she would whimper and crawl along the ground and try to kiss your feet. So no one went near her unless they needed her medicines. They didn't even bother to feel sorry for her.

With Buzz flitting behind her, Heather went down through the birch grove until they came to sour black ground where reeds and rushes grew almost head high. Beyond the reeds and rushes spread the swamp, a glittering waste of frothy scum that looked firm and was, around the edges, where it was only a shallow surface of mud on a ledge of stone. But in its center it was very deep and would swallow up a cow or even an acorn dropped on its surface.

Heather stood gazing over this evil marsh glinting and stinking in the sun. Buzz pulled at her skirt. "I'm scared," she whimpered. "I don't want you to go any closer."

Beyond a small dusty dooryard, the Swampwife's hut huddled among the reeds like a rat's nest. The door was open. No one seemed to be inside.

Heather had almost decided to turn back with Buzz when they heard the slosh of someone's walking in mud. They hid and peered out through the reeds. The old woman was walking in the swamp. Where she walked the mud was no deeper than her ankles. But where she poked with a long stick it was very deep. She was feeling about with the stick, poking in one place then another, looking for something. On one thin wrist she wore two muddy bracelets of heavy gold.

Heather remembered her father's saying that here the Sun People had camped many years ago. Into this swamp they had thrown sacrifices to the sun. She stepped into the dooryard and called, "Swampwife! I want some herbs to stop my bee stings from itching!" She was sure this poor old woman had not told the Sun People about the tree of Oakwood.

Slowly, the withered old crone came up out of the swamp. She put her muddy stick carefully on the ground. She spat on the gold bracelets on her arm and wiped them clean on her skirt. Jingling them on her knobbly wrist, she held them out to Heather and whined, "Are these what you've come to take from me?"

"No."

The old creature smiled. She had no teeth. "I have much prettier things inside. Come in, Heather Good-shade, and I'll give you anything you want. Come in, come in."

Heather did not want to go inside. But she did. She was curious about this strange old woman, and sorry for her.

The hut was full of hanging bunches of dried leaves and seeds and burrs and berries. It smelled sweet and dry, spicy and smoky. Mixed with so many perfumes, even the musky smell of the marsh was not unpleasant.

"Why have you come to see me?" asked the old woman.

Heather hesitated for a moment, and then said, "To find out if you hate the tree."

The Swampwife stared at her. "Who has said I do?"

"No one."

"Then why do you ask me?"

"Because the Sun People are coming. There may be a war. They have a secret friend who has told them about our tree.

The old woman leaped up and screamed, "Your slave, your bad little slave! She has the marks on her!"

"It is not Buzz," said Heather quietly. "I know she scared you almost to death. But she is as much afraid of the Sun People as you are."

The Swampwife shuddered and clinked her bracelets together nervously. "I knew they'd come back. I've been waiting for them a long time. They threw my husband into this swamp. He's still there. Someday I'll find him."

Weeping, she crushed a few brittle leaves and sprinkled them on the embers of her fire. A thread of blue smoke curled up and filled the hut with a strange, sweet smell. As she sat over the fire breathing the smoke, her eyes opened wider and wider. She stared past Heather as if she were seeing creatures from another world crowding in through the door. Heather could not see these visitors, but when she felt them brush past her like cobwebs, she knew the smoke had begun to poison her too, and she ran outside.

After a moment the strangeness left her. She found Buzz huddled among the reeds. Together they went up through the birch wood into the meadow.

"Weren't you scared to be in there with her?" asked Buzz.

"Mostly I was sad. You must never frighten her again. Promise me you'll never frighten her again!"

Buzz looked away as if she hadn't heard. "That old toad-eater hates me. She thinks I'll tell what she has in her house. Did she fix your bee stings?"

"I forgot about them," said Heather.

All at once they began to itch again.

THE FOREST PEOPLE ate their breakfast any time they felt hungry: a cup of milk or berry juice sweetened with honey or a few nuts or roots they happened to find as they went about their morning chores. At noon they ate inside their houses. It was almost like a religious service. When anyone spoke, it was softly, and only about pleasant things.

Chief Goodshade always spoke softly. He was a very calm person, tall and straight, blue-eyed, with fair hair down to his broad shoulders. He moved slowly as powerful men do. He was a good farmer and hunter, and a wise and beloved leader of his village. When he spoke, it was with few words, and they were obeyed.

Buzz ate with the family. At first her manners had not been very good. But Heather's patience and Goodshade's silences had taught her to behave quite well most of the time. This morning she was not thinking about manners. When Reindeer, who was Tree Woman's slave, brought in the pig meat Buzz pushed up the corners of her own eyes in a way that made her look like Reindeer with her fat cheeks and slant eyes. Reindeer, who was good-natured and a little stupid, giggled and spilled food on the elk hide.

But that was not the worst thing Buzz did. When everyone broke off a chunk of bread and bowed and thanked the tree for it, she popped her crust into her mouth, chewed it noisily, and said, "I don't see why a tree has to be thanked for bread. Nothing grows under a tree except moss, and you can't eat moss."

Chief Goodshade and Tree Woman said nothing. Heather turned away, and Buzz realized she had done something wrong again. "Was it because I talked with my mouth full, or what I said?"

Everyone was silent. They helped themselves to meat and cheese and roots and ate solemnly, as if Buzz wasn't there.

"I am sorry," muttered the child. Daintily she nibbled her food. But she wasn't hungry any more, and asked to be excused. "The children are going down to the shore to dig holes in the sand. May I go?"

Heather said quietly, "Mother wants us to gather berries to mix with our honey."

Buzz pouted. "What kind of berries?"

"Cranberries. And marsh myrtle."

Buzz thought for a moment and then smiled. "I'll gather the berries!"

Heather was watching her. "You're planning to scare the Swampwife again, aren't you?"

Buzz did not answer.

Chief Goodshade glanced at his daughter and asked, "Have you been to see the old woman?"

Before Heather could reply, Buzz interrupted, "Yes, she has! She went down there this morning. She doesn't think that old toad-eater is bad!"

"She's not!" cried Heather, and then was sorry she had spoken so loudly.

"Buzz is right," said Goodshade.

"But, Father, I talked to her. A long time ago the Sun People killed her husband. She's still trying to find him in the swamp. It's terribly sad."

"Why did you go down there?" asked her father.

"To get something to put on my bee stings." She hesitated, and then confessed, "And to find out who told the Sun People about our tree. Someone in Oakwood."

"Who?"

"I don't know."

After a moment, Goodshade said, "I think I can guess."

Heather was surprised. She supposed her mother had told him about Wolf Stone. She could see that her father had said all he was going to say.

Buzz was suddenly very hungry, and pleased with herself. She ate all her food and part of Heather's. Waiting carefully until she had swallowed everything, she said sweetly to Tree Woman, "If you'd like to send Reindeer to pick marsh myrtle and cranberries, I'll get some fresh water." She smiled at Heather. "Then you'll know I'm not down there bothering that old witch."

Tree Woman smiled. "You may get the water."

After everyone had stood up, Buzz took a clay jar and lifted it onto her head. Without holding it, with quick floating steps, she walked out toward the spring.

Heather could not understand why her father thought the poor old Swampwife was bad. As if she would ever do anything to help the Sun People!

Goodshade knew what was puzzling his daughter, and said, "The story the old woman told you is not true. Many years ago, when the Sun People camped down there, she was even then not a young woman. She had a good husband. She betrayed him to the sun-priests, who sacrificed him in the swamp. She did this to become the woman of the sun-chief, whose name was Thunder. He was a thin man with angry narrow eyes and a nose like a hawk's beak. She lived with him in his tent of painted skins. He gave her amber and bracelets of bronze and gold. But when Thunder discovered he could not drive his cattle to drink at our spring and would be lucky to escape from our bowmen with his life, he took back all the presents he had given her and threw them into the swamp. There he left her, and there she has lived ever since, fishing up her bangles out of the mud. That is the true story."

Heather sighed. "I can see why she hates the Sun People."

"No one knows what the Swampwife hates or loves," he said.

"Anyway, she couldn't be the person who told Great Elk about our tree."

"True," said Goodshade, "she is not the one."

"You said you know who is."

"I do."

Heather noticed that her mother had gone out and was helping Reindeer in the cooking shelter, and that Blue Wing had come in and was standing in the doorway.

Blue Wing and her father were both looking at her. She knew they had something important to tell her.

"You have wondered," said Goodshade, "who told the Sun People about our tree—who told them first which tree it was not, and then pointed out which tree it was."

"I have wondered," she said.

He spoke softly. "It was you, my daughter."

She was horrified. "That's not true!"

"The son of Great Elk said we should all hide in the forest until the Sun People went away. Is that so?"

"Yes! So they would not discover our tree!"

Goodshade gently took her hand. "If we had gone to hide in the forest, we would have returned to find our god cut into timbers, being made into a ship."

Heather drew her hand away. She shook her head. "No. That can't be true. Wolf Stone would never deceive me."

"He promised to deceive his father."

Goodshade and Blue Wing sat gazing at the floor. They couldn't bear to look at her. Her eyes were deep with hurt.

It was true. Wolf Stone had been curious about the tree she had climbed, with its long curved bough like a ship's keel. He had been curious about it until she had said it was not the tree that was a god. Then, from the mound, he had noticed the tallest of all the oaks in the forest. She couldn't remember if she had told him it was the sacred tree, the tree of power. But he had guessed it was. He had looked at it strangely for a long time.

Everything Blue Wing and her father believed about Wolf Stone seemed to be true. They believed he had only wanted to find the tree. But Heather could not believe this! She would not believe it! Her heart seemed to burst. She ran to her sleeping corner, threw herself down, covered her head with her lambskins, and sobbed.

W HEN Heather had no more strength left to weep,
she lay looking up at the underside of the roof
thatch where a small web of afternoon light danced like
a flame. She wasn't at all curious to know what caused
it. She didn't care. She heard small summer twitterings
outside, but didn't bother to wonder what made them.
Only one steady clicking sound at last tapped through
the emptiness in her mind.

She sat up and saw that the tapping sound was made
by Blue Wing chipping arrow points. He was sitting in

the shade of Littleman's house where he never worked. He was hoping she would notice him and know what he was doing. But she didn't care what he was doing.

She went out and looked around to see what made the ripple of light on her ceiling. It was made by sunlight touching water in the jar Buzz had left beside the door. Heather guessed that Buzz and her mother and Reindeer had gone down to the swamp to gather cranberries and bog myrtle. If Buzz did scare the old woman again, it didn't matter.

She went over and sat on the ground a little way from Blue Wing and watched him. He glanced at her without saying anything, and went on with his work. He gripped a core of flint and gave its flat edge one sharp tap with a hammer stone. A thin flake split off, and he caught it in the air. He looked at it carefully, held it in a scrap of leather and with a prong of deer antler pressed small flakes off its edges. At last the stone was shaped and sharp and pointed. He chipped a few small flakes off the wide end, leaving two little ears, and there in his hand lay a perfect point. He tossed it on a small pile of others he had finished, put his tools aside, and waited for Heather to speak if she wanted to.

She sat looking at the ground, drawing circles in the dust.

After a while he said, "I suppose you know . . . I have spoken to your father."

"Other people have told me. But not you."

"You knew it though."

She nodded.

He picked up the flint core and started to knock off another flake.

"Have I hurt you?" she asked, still drawing circles with her finger.

He smiled. "Only by taking too long to grow up." He seemed a little angry. "You know I've already shot and skinned a red deer. You must have guessed what I was building out by the meadow. And then—this boy came along. You didn't tell me about him."

Heather flushed. "He's not a boy. He's as old as you are. And as strong. And taller. He makes things, too. Out of bronze. You should see the sword he made."

"Can he split a bee in flight with it?"

She didn't answer, knowing that no one could.

Blue Wing sifted his arrow points through his fingers. "Have you noticed the hides are down over most of the doors? Do you know why?"

"No."

"Because the men who went out to warn the villages are back, and sleeping. All except Littleman. Tonight there will be a meeting of the chiefs. By morning our tree will be guarded by archers with their chins and cheeks painted red. No one knows when their stone bees will start to fly."

Heather said stubbornly, "By morning the Sun People will be gone without even knowing we are here."

Blue Wing made a grunting bearlike sound, and she cried out, "That is all Wolf Stone wants! And that is what will happen! Unless you and my father start a war."

Blue Wing's eyebrows went up, and she said angrily, "Is it so impossible to believe someone could love me so much?"

He frowned. "The spring and the tree both told us not to trust him."

"*I* trust him!" she said. "Even if I'm wrong, even if he laughs at me for trusting him—I will still trust him." Her eyes filled with tears. "I may never see him again in this world, but I will always love him." It was the first time she had admitted, even to herself, that she loved him.

She could see how much she had hurt Blue Wing, and was sorry. "Where is my father?" she asked wearily.

"Trying to find out why Littleman hasn't come back." Blue Wing looked at her with narrowed eyes. "Littleman went out past the camp of the Sun People to let them capture and question him. When he comes back—if he ever does—we may know what Great Elk will do now that he knows our archers are ready for war. What you said is so. By morning the Sun People may be gone. But not because they don't know where to find us."

While he was talking he had finished another arrow point. He tossed it with the others and said, "Which of these bees, I wonder, will be the one to sting Wolf Stone?"

GOODSHADE stood on the highest of the sandy hills, watching for Littleman, hoping to see his small hobbling figure coming across the heath. All he saw was a wilderness wavering in heat, and a haze of dust over the camp in the distance.

When he returned to the village, he was surprised to see the painted hide down over Littleman's doorway. He stooped and went inside.

Littleman was so old that no one remembered his real name. He was bent and wrinkled as a withered berry.

77

But there was no man in all the forest so brave. It had been his own plan to walk across the heath to Birdsong Village, then to return close to the camp of the Sun People and let them capture him.

He lay on the floor of his house, grimy with sweat and dust, his small body slashed with red welts. He was so tired he could hardly keep his eyes open. But as he spoke to Goodshade he smiled. "They captured me, as I thought they would. They took me to Great Elk and questioned me, as I hoped they would. I refused to tell them where I had been and why—until they beat me. Now they know what we want them to know, that our archers are painting their cheeks and chins red. Now I think they will go peacefully on their way."

"Are they armed with bows?"

"I saw only swords."

"Did they speak about our tree?"

"Yes. It seems our tree is famous even to the edges of the world. They believe a ship built of it could never be sunk. I told them I had never heard of such a tree."

"Did they believe you?"

"Great Elk did. He gave me a drink of ale from his gold cup and sent me home. I left there walking to the east. But not alone. I had followers as sly and clever as wolves. I lost them in the brambles where I crept through animal tunnels. When I reached the long wood,

I turned north again and came home." Littleman sighed and smiled. "It was a pleasant journey."

"Sleep well," murmured Goodshade. He went out, dropping the wolf hide across the doorway.

Troll Tamer and his priests were chanting in their great tent made of white skins scrawled with pale red and yellow magic symbols. It stood near the great sun-disk, apart from the clutter of wagons and piles of firewood and stores of food and scattered tents that made up the crowded camp.

The most colorful tent was Great Elk's with its two tall poles topped by the sun-whitened, antlered skulls of elk. It was set up not far from the brown lake, near a few scattered pine trees from which the lower branches had been hacked off for fuel. This tent was made of untrimmed elk hides with the ears and tails left on like tassels. Both the tent and the awning stretched out before it were painted with bold black and red and yellow designs of warriors in battle and hunters in pursuit of animals.

The chief sat in the shade of his awning in a painted wooden chair he had carried with him for many years. He was drinking ale from a cup of solid gold. He was a heavy man, with a short grizzled beard. He seldom turned his head, but his shrewd eyes missed very little.

There was no land he had ever wanted to see that he had not seen. There was nothing he had ever wanted to do that he had not done. When he was a young man he had lived in the eastern grasslands where he learned how to make bronze and shape it into swords. These he had traded for the daughters of chieftains, until he was related to so many powerful tribes that his own chieftain tried to kill him, which was foolish of the old man because Great Elk killed him first, and all his children. All except his prettiest daughter, who became the mother of Wolf Stone.

Now, Great Elk was growing old. He could no longer ride a horse, and was tired of jolting about the world in a wagon. He had traveled and fought and enjoyed himself everywhere. He had visited towns built on lakes and looted and burned them. He had fought slant-eyed horsemen and won for himself a fine herd of horses and cattle. Now he was moving slowly to the north, his people mounted or on foot, his tents and goods in wagons. He was moving slowly to the north with a new purpose.

Beside the blue southern sea he had seen ships owned by Pharaohs and kings, but had never cared to travel in a ship until he heard of the tree of power. When he heard that a ship built of the wood of this tree could never be sunk, he thought it would be pleasant in his old age to float comfortably about the seas destroying the power of kings. When he died, he would leave his ship to his son Wolf Stone, who could then become the richest and mightiest chieftain of all the rulers of the world. That was the dream behind his purpose.

On the ground beside Greak Elk sat a man with a narrow, hungry face. He wore leather breeches and a cape of tattered skins. There was little flesh on his bones, but he was strong, with large nervous hands. His name was Eagle. He had been found starving in the snowy mountains, trying to reach the sea. He swore that he was a chief, or had been until his brother stole his wives, his ship and his treasure and sold him into slavery. On his forehead he wore the marks of the Sun People. He wanted only to reach a sea with trees near it, to build a ship and sail it against his brother. He promised half of all he once owned to anyone who would help him find the sea. This was agreeable to Greak Elk.

Now, after two years, Eagle could at last smell the sea, not far away, beyond a forest; and he was wild to begin building his ship, using any tree at all for its timbers. "One sound oak properly curved is as good as another," he said.

Great Elk roared as he had many times before, "The timbers for this ship must be cut from the tree of power! Now keep your clacking beak shut until we find it!"

Eagle did not believe in such a tree and would not be silent. "No one else in this tribe knows how to build a ship. My father said he had once seen the tree of power not far to the south of his land." He smiled insolently. "That might be about here. I could point to any tree in the forest and say, 'That is the one!' You couldn't prove me wrong."

"I will know when we find it," growled Great Elk and drank his ale.

The chief's angry silence was broken by the soothing voice of his head priest, who stood before the awning. He had been led there by two of his attendants who touched his elbows and now stepped back. "Great Elk is right," said Troll Tamer. "The tree must be found. But Eagle is also right. There is no power in the tree. It is only a great vegetable. It must be found, and destroyed, cut into wood for any use. Better burned. The people who worship it must be destroyed. Cut down in battle. Better, burned. Or made into useful slaves."

In his long white cape and cap, Troll Tamer was almost invisible in the glittering light. He knew the ways of the sun and could tame it with dances and lurs. He knew the time for such rites and ceremonies. But he cared nothing about people or what they did, as long as they danced and chanted at the proper times. He loved only the sun.

Great Elk did not deny Troll Tamer's skill in taming the sun. But the chief had seen many things that a priest's eyes, gazing always above the earth, could not see. He believed in the magic of the tree and intended to be sure of two things—that Troll Tamer did not burn it, and that the ship Eagle built was built of its unsinkable timbers. Great Elk said nothing of this to either of them.

A young warrior had stepped between the poles of the awning and was waiting for the chief to notice him. When Great Elk nodded to him, the young man said, "We lost the little man. We followed him as far as a wall of brambles where he vanished into animal tunnels too small for us to crawl through."

"Is that Oxtenstar?" asked Troll Tamer without turning to him.

"Yes," said the warrior nervously.

"You were told not to lose the little man."

"He crept away like a rabbit."

"What should you have done?" asked the priest.

Oxenstar clenched his hands to keep them from trembling. "I don't know."

"Burn the brambles! Roast him like a rabbit!"

Great Elk grunted and drank a swig of ale. "How would that have told us where he went?"

"I know where he went," said the priest. "To the tree."

"He knew nothing about the tree!" shouted the chief.

Troll Tamer was silent.

Great Elk started to speak again. Instead, he drained his cup, tossed the lees from it, and dismissed Oxenstar.

As the young warrior moved to go, Troll Tamer pointed a long thin finger at him and said, "Scourge him with brambles!"

Two priests, armed under their robes, stepped out from behind the tent and led Oxenstar away.

Great Elk sighed. "That boy is a good captain, and one of my sons."

"You have too many sons," said Troll Tamer.

Great Elk glared at the priest. Then he grumbled, "Why would you doubt that frightened little man who told us nothing until he was beaten, and yet believe an old witch who comes mumbling to you in the night?"

From gazing at the sun, Troll Tamer turned his face toward the chief. It seemed a calm, kindly face—until you saw that his eyes were sightless, hard and white like stone, without pupils. "I believe the Swampwife," he said, "because she hates the tree. Tonight she will lead Knife and Longfire to it. Before another day, Eagle's men will have it felled and in ten days cut into timbers."

Great Elk roared with laughter. "You hear that, Eagle! Tomorrow you fell the tree! When the Forest People shoot you full of arrows, pay no attention to them!"

"If it cannot be cut," said the priest, "it will be burned."

Great Elk's face turned an angry red. "You would do well to believe the little man when he said the forest archers are painting their cheeks and chins red."

"That I believe," said Troll Tamer. "But I am a man of peace. I leave the fighting to you."

The chief's small eyes narrowed. "A hundred days from now," he said, "we will take the tree, without battle, and without interference from you." Troll Tamer's long fingers twitched. And Great Elk growled, "The line of a blood curse is drawn between us. See that you stay on your side of it!"

Troll Tamer gestured toward his two attendant priests, Knife and Longfire, who stepped forward, touched his elbows, and led him away.

Great Elk remained motionless until Troll Tamer was out of sight. Then, with the back of his hand he wiped a dew of cold sweat off his forehead.

Eagle still sat beside him, picking his teeth, as if the hatred he had seen flash between the priest and the chief was no concern of his.

Great Elk's laugh was like a snarl. "I should have poisoned him long ago. He would poison me now except that he knows if I die, so will he; and if he dies, so will I. That is the curse we have put on each other."

Eagle snorted with disgust. "A curse on all curses!" He stood up lazily. Leaning his awkward limbs against a pole of the awning, he looked at Great Elk with open scorn. "So you intend to take the tree without a war a hundred days from now! What makes you think you'll be alive a hundred days from now? Your greatest enemies aren't the priests, but the captains, most of them your sons. What did you do to protect Oxenstar from being scourged? Nothing. He'd be glad to see you and that blind white serpent both dead!"

Great Elk smiled. "The captains will soon be more eager to deal with Troll Tamer before he roasts them all like rabbits."

"Every day they are ready to deal with Troll Tamer," sneered Eagle. "Then the lurs bray like donkeys, and like donkeys they dance and sweat in terror."

"Don't make me angry, Eagle," said Great Elk. "I know you are the only man in my tribe who can build a ship. But where is your army? Who will destroy your brother and take back your wives and your treasure? Do you think my warriors would follow you into battle?" He laughed shortly. "Some of my sons, as you say, have no love for me. But all of them know I have no lost battles behind me. I will command the ship. When I have captured your treasure, you will pay me half of it."

Eagle still slouched against the tent pole, but he seemed less confident. "Why do you wait a hundred days, then, to take the tree without a war? Are you afraid of the Forest People?"

"Only a fool would send swordsmen against archers in a forest. In a hundred days I will take the tree without a blow except that of your ax."

"You know that, do you?" sneered Eagle.

"I know it!" roared Great Elk, banging his empty cup on the arm of his chair. His slave came out of the tent and filled the cup with ale. The chief drained it in one draft.

The veins on Eagle's neck bulged, and the hollows under his cheekbones twitched.

Great Elk laughed at his anger. "I know every thought in your ugly head, Eagle. Not all talk is to the ear. Your big thumbs tell me clearly they crave to strangle me. But you can see this bull's neck of mine would be a handful. Now you are wondering if this gold cup is heavy enough to crack my skull. But how would you get hold of it? An ax might serve you better. Or would it? Once the bronze tasted blood, no other ax would ever again bite wood for you. A flint ax? But where would you get a flint ax? From the Forest People?"

Eagle wet his dry lips with a flick of his tongue, and Great Elk chuckled. "Now you are thinking about the witches' way. But you know my slave has a dog's nose and can sniff the smell of any poison made of stone or leaves or the spit of snakes. Also he tastes everything before I eat or drink. Only two men in his position have had the misfortune to save my life. So, what other means can you think of to kill me?"

Eagle muttered, "I know one weapon you fear—an arrow."

Great Elk was amused. "I have on my body nine arrow wounds. None more serious than the bite of a bee. In open battle archery is a boy's game. I will admit, I don't care to fight an invisible army among trees. But I have no intention of going among trees."

"Where will you go then to find the tree of power?" snarled Eagle.

"I have found it. Now go away and let me live at least until I've destroyed your brother for you. On that day, stab me with a sword. It will be much easier than paying me my share of your treasure."

Eagle winced. Again the chief laughed. "Swords displease you? Why? Perhaps I can guess. Because a sword is useless in your clumsy grasp. Isn't that why your brother despised you and robbed you and cast you out? You're too awkward to wield so subtle a tool. Now go away! Do your hating out of my sight!"

Flushed with fury, Eagle went out to the quarter of the camp where the slaves lived huddled in filth. There he called together those men he had trained to be carpenters. They squatted about him in the shade of wagons, waiting for his command. He had promised these dozen or so slaves their freedom when his ship was built. They had already heard that Great Elk wanted to build it of some magic tree that could only be taken by war. Their faces were ugly with impatience.

Eagle looked out at the long wood where the little man had vanished. Slowly his eyes moved northward to the hills with a dark wave of trees beyond. "That is where the village would be," he said. Then he called to a thin, sallow slave whose clever fingers could plait a cord of horsehair or a rope of thongs or the peeled bark of briars. "Goatbeard," growled Eagle, "let me see that black string you are forever twisting!"

Goatbeard came forward with light steps like a dancer and smiled, holding a black cord by its two ends.

Eagle took the cord and tested its strength. "If Great Elk runs us into a war, you might have the pleasure of using this on him. First, show us how it works."

"Gladly," said Goatbeard with a smile.

Eagle looked over the slaves crouching beside the

wagons. A little apart sat a man known as Dustyfoot. Of all the grimy crew he was the dirtiest and most docile. Although he fumbled willingly at any work, each day his hands were becoming more knotted and stiff. Eagle remembered when Dustyfoot was captured, only a year ago. For his youthful arrogance he was wracked and beaten. But still he laughed at torture. Until, after one long night in Troll Tamer's tent, he had come out wincing and mindless as a tame animal. He had never laughed again. Now with his stiffening hands he was of little use to Eagle, who handed the slim string to Goatbeard and said, "Try it on Dustyfoot."

The delicate business was quickly over. Eagle shook his head. "No, Goatbeard. At ten paces Great Elk would smell you. He would turn and laugh at your pretty dance." Again he gazed out at the sandy hills. "There's a village beyond those hills among the biggest trees in the wood and near the sea. I think I will go there to buy a tree, a good keel-tree. And perhaps a stone ax. Or a bow. Or some strange herb as sweet as mead. Something to persuade Great Elk that one sound oak is as good as another." To his slaves he shouted, "Tomorrow we start to build! Sharpen your axes!" He walked away, loose-limbed, shambling and awkward, toward the long wood that led to the north.

Returning from the peace and gentleness of Heather's village, Wolf Stone was unhappily aware of the barbaric squalor of his own camp. His small tent had been set up not far from his father's, not far from the lake. But the smell of stale muddy water and of the cattle that drank there sickened him. And so, working quietly and alone while the camp slept, he moved his tent and his forge, his anvil, his ingots of tin and copper, and his tools to the only high ground near-by. This sandy elevation had been avoided because some-one had killed a snake there, among the rocks and boulders scattered over it. Here, after many trips back and forth, Wolf Stone set up his tent.

The sky had begun to pale before he sank wearily down on his bed of skins.

His mind was weighted with worry. He had promised to deceive his father into leading his tribe past Heather's village. Now he knew he could not do this. Heather had become the light of his whole life, and he could not cloud it with deception. If he had to die to save her, he would die. But how to do what he had promised to do was beyond the reach of his weary mind.

It was midday when Oxenstar found him and wakened him. The young captain was weeping, not because of the bleeding wounds that striped his face, but from anger. His voice trembled. "The time has come, Wolf Stone, when you must listen to me. A hundred warriors are weeping with my angry tears and speaking with my voice as I tell you we must kill Troll Tamer!"

Wolf Stone leaped up, shaking the darkness out of his head. He noticed his brother's bleeding face.

"What he has done to me doesn't matter," said Oxenstar. "We must kill him because he is making our good sun into a demon. Our god in the sun is a dying slave. We must save him, or we will all rot in darkness and be eaten by the roots of trees. We must kill Troll Tamer!"

"You know that Great Elk will die with him," said Wolf Stone.

"We know. Great Elk will die. But the sun will be free again and will take him up to the land we all come from! Do you want to be nibbled away by worms under the earth?"

Wolf Stone shuddered. He held his head in his hands. "I don't want Great Elk to die."

Oxenstar continued more quietly, "We would like to tell him we will accept you as our chieftain after him."

Wolf Stone cried out, "I will not let you kill him!"

Blood was oozing into Oxenstar's mouth. He wiped it away and said, "Then we must do what must be done without your knowing of it, without Great Elk's knowing of it. When he dies, then I and not you will take his place. This is the word of the captains. We give you until tomorrow to choose." Oxenstar turned and walked out of the tent.

GREAT ELK paced slowly back and forth under his awning. His limbs moved heavily, but his small eyes twinkled as he planned the way he would take the tree without a battle. First, of course, he had to find the tree. As Eagle had said, anyone might call any tree the tree of power. But Great Elk knew how to be sure. He would make the Forest People themselves point it out.

He shouted for Wolf Stone to be sent to him.

His slave nodded toward the lake. The chief looked out and saw that Wolf Stone's tent was gone.

Rumbling like a bull, with massive, savage power, he moved out toward the lake where his son's tent had been.

Glancing over the dust, he realized from footmarks and the scratches of dragged tent poles, that the boy had moved himself away from the lake, away from the smell of the cattle, which even Great Elk had to admit was not pleasant.

Glancing in the direction taken by the dragged poles, he saw the tent at some distance on a rocky rise among boulders. Slowly he walked up the slope.

Wolf Stone had rolled up one side of his tent to catch any breath of air that stirred in the quivering heat. He sat watching his father trudge up the hillside, slowly, like an old man. Only a few years ago Great Elk had seemed young. In those days, shouting and commanding, he had been the boy's constant companion. They had hunted and sung together, or worked at the forge and anvil together.

Now Great Elk was an old man. He came into the tent, sweating and out of breath. He sat down on a lamb skin and noticed at once a fresh stain of blood on the fleece. "I see that Oxenstar has been here. Did he ask you to kill Troll Tamer?"

"He knew I wouldn't."

"Because you believe killing him would kill me too?"

Wolf Stone nodded.

Great Elk smiled. "Do you believe Troll Tamer has taken over all my authority?"

"That is how it seems."

Still smiling, the chief said, "Don't believe it. What power I yield to the priest is of no importance. Our people must dance to stay limber for battle when there is no battle. They must chant themselves hoarse to keep them from growling amongst themselves. There is only one reason I haven't slit Troll Tamer's throat myself. Who would lead the sun-dances and the chanting? I have no desire to. I enjoy the ceremony most while dozing in my tent." He chuckled. "As for Troll Tamer's curse, that is my armor against his ambition. He believes in curses. I don't. Do you believe I will die when he dies?"

"Not if you don't believe it," said Wolf Stone.

Great Elk was content. "Now let me tell you how I will find the tree of power."

The boy was silent, his face hot with shame. If his father should ask if he had found the tree, he could not lie. He would have to say that he had. But Great Elk did not ask. "This is how we will find it," he said, making marks on the earth floor. "For one change of the moon, from full to full again, we will stay camped here by the lake, herding our animals to the south, hunting our game in the southern woods. The tree lies to the north beyond those sandy hills. Each day we will celebrate with games and dancing and chanting before the sun-disk. The lurs will sound at break of day, at noon, and at sunset. Soon we will see children watching us from the hills. Soon the forest archers will become tired of holding the feathers of their arrows up to their ears. Their women will become tired of bringing them food. They will go back to their farming and hunting. Then you, my son, will follow those who watch us from the hills. You will go as a friend to their villages, with presents for the children. Soon they will show you a tree, only one tree, guarded by forest archers. That will be the tree of power." Great Elk was watching his son's face closely. "Will you do this?" he asked.

Wolf Stone nodded. His heart was beating wildly. He forced his voice to be calm as he asked, "How can we take the tree without a war?"

His father smiled. "That, I will tell you later."

When Great Elk had gone, Wolf Stone sat alone in his tent, staring out over the camp of his people. When the lurs sounded and everyone ran out to dance and chant before the sun-disk, he still sat in his tent. His heart ached because he knew that when night fell he would betray his father. He would go to Heather and tell her the tree of power must not be guarded, but only the tall curved tree where she had found the bees.

THAT NIGHT the chiefs of all the forest villages met under the tree of Oakwood. No fires were lit for sacrifice. The moon, close to full, surrounded the tree's shadow with a glimmering wall of light. Close to the gray trunk sat the chiefs, murmuring uneasily. They were aware of each other only as darker shadows, as if they were ghosts.

Goodshade spoke to them in his gentle voice. "Before another day has passed, the Sun People may be gone on their way to the north. The lesson our fathers taught those earlier men of swords may still be remembered.

But that tribe wanted only water for their cattle. The chieftain of this tribe has another desire. He has heard that this tree above us—and it may be so—if built into a ship, could never be sunk by any storm in any sea. It is our wise and gentle god this chieftain wants."

"How will he find our tree?" asked one of the chiefs.

"He has found it," said Goodshade.

"Then we must guard it."

"We will guard our tree," they all said, and messengers were sent to summon every archer in the forest to surround and protect the sacred tree of Oakwood.

O LD FANG and his two half-grown puppies were the dogs in Oakwood. As soon as the puppies were weaned, their mother had run away to join a wolf pack. Fang looked like a wolf, a tattered old wolf, but he was called Fang only because he doddered around wagging his tail and showing his teeth in a big smile. He was perfectly useless. But everyone loved him. His puppies were just like him, good-natured and useless. There was only one thing about them that was annoying. When the moon was close to full, when there was no wind and the night was still, the three dogs would sit out on the bare ground between the houses and howl.

It was that kind of a night, with crickets chirping like a tide in the stillness, like the breathing of the earth. The moon was high, but for once the dogs weren't howling. Perhaps they sensed, as Buzz did, that not one person in the whole silent village was asleep. Goodshade and Blue Wing and the archers had all gone, silent as shadows, out to the tree.

Heather was pretending to be asleep. She was thinking about Wolf Stone and praying there would be no war.

Buzz was restless. It was too quiet! On tiptoe she went outside to see why the dogs weren't howling. She found them lying dead on the bare ground between the houses. They had been eating a rabbit. This was strange, because they were too spoiled and lazy to catch game. In the moonlight, Buzz looked closely at the half-eaten rabbit. It had been cut open and stuffed with dry, black, brittle leaves. The Swampwife had poisoned the dogs to keep them from howling at the moon, from waking and warning people that the Sun People were coming!

The child went inside and tearfully whispered to Heather what had happened. They went out and looked sadly at poor old dead Fang and his two puppies, and Buzz muttered savagely, "Now you know how bad she is! I wish someone would poison her!"

While they were standing there, an archer stepped out of the shadow of the forest and stood watching them. Even that far away Heather could tell it was Blue Wing; he looked so much like a bear armed with a bow.

When he came and stared down at the dead dogs, he said wearily, "This proves the Sun People have found us." He looked sadly at Heather. "After this, do you still trust Wolf Stone?"

In a low voice she said, "The Swampwife poisoned them! If you don't believe me, come with me and I'll prove it! She has black leaves just like these in her house. I'll show you!"

"My orders," he said, "are to guard the tree."

She turned away. He held her arm and said, "Don't go down there!"

She shrugged away from him. He still held her arm. Buzz slapped at him and said, "You let her go!" He released her. The child took Heather's hand, and they walked away across the meadow. Blue Wing could not follow them. He loped silently back to his post in the forest.

Heather and Buzz sat in the shadow of the great stones on the mound, looking out over hills that were like waves caught in the moonlight and held motionless. Silence everywhere seemed to be listening for the movement of men with swords.

Then they saw what they expected and dreaded to see. On top of one of the hills a white form arose, then another. Two men stood there, almost invisible.

"Sun-priests!" whispered Buzz. She shuddered.

The white forms vanished, appearing in a moment below the hills. Beyond the field they came steadily on toward the village, crouching low as they passed the bramble hedge, gliding swiftly over the meadow, disappearing into the birch wood.

Heather and Buzz followed them down through the birch grove toward the swamp. There, hiding among the reeds, they watched as two powerful men, drawing swords from under their robes, moved cautiously to the door of the Swampwife's hut and looked in. A deep voice rumbled, "She's not there." They looked around the clearing nervously.

From the far side of the swamp came a croaking sound that might have been a frog. It was the Swampwife laughing as she stood ankle-deep in mud. All around her spread a glistening green moon-silvered pool of slime.

Longfire called in his deep voice, "What are you doing out there?"

The old woman jingled the gold bracelets on her thin arms and cackled, "Finding treasure. Come and take what you want!" Moonlight glowed on a muddy breastplate of amber nuggets that covered her flat chest.

Longfire growled, "Those are offerings to the sun.

We cannot take them. Come out now and lead us to the tree as you promised Troll Tamer you would."

The Swampwife lifted the amber breastplate over her head and threw it toward them. It fell a few feet from the shore where it lay lightly on the surface of the marsh. Knife gazed at this treasure with greedy eyes. Then a pair of golden bracelets splashed almost at his feet. The scum scarcely covered them.

Knife took off his white robe, placed his sword on it, and stepped out carefully on the slimy, slippery stone. His armor creaked as he squatted down to pick up the bracelets. He stood up and hefted them, and looked at the amber lying only a step away.

Behind the reeds, Buzz whispered, "He doesn't know that amber floats!" Heather gripped her arm to make her be quiet.

But Longfire had heard Buzz's whispering. He turned and, holding his sword before him, moved toward the reeds. Behind him Knife gasped. And Longfire heard a gurgling sound and a bursting of bubbles. When he looked back at the swamp, he saw only the amber bobbing slightly as a dark hollow in the mud smoothed out to a glistening surface of slime. Knife was gone. Across the marsh, the Swampwife croaked and stamped her feet in a dance of glee. Longfire gazed at her in horror.

Suddenly Buzz ran out past him, buzzing like an angry hornet, and what her buzzing had done before to

the Swampwife happened again. The old woman became rigid as stone. She fell into the deepest part of the
swamp and sank, and bubbles burst out of the mud, flashing silver sparks under the moon.

When the child saw what she had done, she gasped.
The old creature's evil croaking had made her buzz without meaning to! The sun-priest stood gazing at the child,
panting with fear. She ran back toward the reeds where
Heather was hiding.

Longfire moved cautiously after Buzz, thrusting his
sword out before him like a snake's tongue. She vanished,
and he leaped after her, mowing down the reeds and
rushes and roaring hoarsely, "Witches!"

Wolf Stone listened. He was standing below the
mound in a shadow the moon cast of its stones, wondering how to call Heather out of her dark, silent house when
he heard the distant, deep voice roaring, and he ran down
toward the swamp. When he came out of the birch wood,
he found Heather and Buzz crouching beside the path,
a robed sun-priest towering over them, lifting his sword
to strike!

Longfire was startled to see Wolf Stone advancing,
drawing his sword. Backing into the courtyard, he tore off
his white robe and pitched it to one side. With his eyes on
Wolf Stone's eyes, he shifted the weight of his armor,
took a firm grip on his sword, and struck. The blow
missed, and Wolf Stone rushed at the priest. Their

swords clashed, slid upward along the blades and locked at the cross guards. Surprised by the boy's strength, Longfire bared his teeth, his free hand groping for his dagger. Suddenly Wolf Stone's blade was not there, and the priest fell forward headlong, his sword clattering out of his hand.

Quickly whipping the trampled robe over Longfire's head, the boy lashed its belt tightly about the priest's throat. With a stifled roar, Longfire stumbled to his feet, clawing at the belt that was strangling him.

Tapping his sword point on Longfire's breastplate, Wolf Stone nudged him backward, step by step, into the shallow mud of the marsh. "Stop!" he said sharply, and then asked, "Why were you about to kill those girls?"

The priest's voice was muffled, his breathing a painful gasping. "They are witches. Forest witches. The Swampwife was a witch. Now she's drowned. Knife is drowned."

Wolf Stone glanced at the amber floating on the surface of the swamp. He reached out with his sword and picked it out of the dripping slime.

Longfire sank weakly to his knees.

"Why do you hate me?" asked Wolf Stone quietly.

"I don't, I swear I don't!"

"But you hate my father."

"No! I pity the old man."

"Then why don't you free him from Troll Tamer?"

"I've tried to. But Troll Tamer knows. He always

knows." Unable to breathe, he fell over into the shallow mud.

Wolf Stone quickly cut the belt twisted about the priest's throat, unwound the suffocating robe, and helped him up out of the swamp.

Longfire lay on the ground, gasping. At last he stood up weakly, and Wolf Stone asked, "Do you believe Great Elk will die when Troll Tamer dies?"

The priest shuddered. "That is why I can do nothing."

Wolf Stone tossed him the amber breastplate and said, "Take this to Great Elk as a present from me."

Longfire picked up his robe, and Knife's robe, and folded them around the amber. He found his sword and sheathed it. With a puzzled glance at Wolf Stone, he turned and walked up the path through the reeds. In terror, Buzz ran before him.

When the priest was gone, Heather went to Wolf Stone. Their hands met. They stood in silence in the peaceful moonlight. "He would have killed Buzz and me," she said softly. "You were brave."

He shook his head. "Not brave enough to speak to my father. I tried to. I couldn't. I couldn't lie to him. But now—now I know how to keep him from finding your tree." He turned away and said gruffly, "Let him find the wrong one. Guard the tree where you found the bees. Let him make a ship of that."

Heather could see how it hurt him to betray his father. "Will you tell my father what you have told me?" she asked. "This time I think he will believe you."

He nodded.

A MESSENGER had been sent into the forest to summon
Goodshade. Tree Woman sleepily lit rushlights
and placed them about the walls of the room. Heather
and Wolf Stone sat on the elk skin, waiting. When foot-
steps rustled outside, the boy and the girl stood up.

Goodshade stooped under the doorway and stood for
a moment looking at the slender young man standing
beside his daughter. He nodded to them, they sat down,
and he seated himself opposite them. Blue Wing came
in, almost unnoticed, and stood beside the door, bow in
hand, an arrow ready to meet the string.

"If you have words for me, son of Great Elk," said the Chieftain of Oakwood, "speak them."

Wolf Stone's voice was soft with respect. "My first word will make you understand all the others. I love Heather. Do you believe me?"

The chief gazed at him for a moment, and nodded.

"My second word is about my father. He has lived a long life of bluster and deception and warfare. Not even I know when he will be kind or cruel. Now, in his old age he has only one ambition—to leave me, after his death, a ship that can never be sunk. He wants me to conquer kings and become the most powerful chieftain in the world. He respects no law but his own. He has grown tired of our god who is the sun. Can you believe I love such a father?"

Again Goodshade nodded.

"My third word is that I have no wish to become chief of his tribe after him, or to conquer, or to be rich and powerful. When Great Elk dies, Oxenstar will become chief of the Sun People. Then, I would like to return to this village and marry Heather and live here as you do, as one of you. I would like to make things of bronze, which is my craft."

Goodshade asked quietly, "What would you make of bronze?"

Wolf Stone showed the bracelets on his arms. "Ornaments like these."

After a moment, the Chief of the Forest People said, "We do not wear ornaments. Anything more beautiful than it needs to be speaks of pride. Anything we prize too much we give to our gods."

Wolf Stone had never before heard of this way of thinking. He felt a little angry and ashamed.

Goodshade sensed the boy's feelings and smiled. "I am told you know a way to keep your father from destroying our tree. What should we do?"

Wolf Stone spoke hurriedly, not knowing what might offend these strange people. "Make him believe some other tree is your god."

"We have no skill in deception," said the chief a little coldly. "Perhaps you will tell us how to deceive Great Elk."

The boy felt himself blushing. "In your forest," he said, "there is one tree perfectly shaped for a ship's keel. If my father finds only that tree guarded, he will think it is the tree of power."

Goodshade thought for a moment before he spoke. "There are two things I don't understand. First, how would Great Elk discover the wrong tree?"

"He would send out scouts who would believe the guarded tree to be the sacred one."

"And our god, would we leave him unguarded?"

"Yes. And unnoticed."

Goodshade smiled sadly. "What would your scouts

believe when they noticed moss growing under the guarded tree, and yet under another tree, unguarded, the earth beaten to dust by dancing? What could your father say except that we had tried to deceive him? Also, if we left our holy tree without protection, one man clever with bronze knives could quickly girdle its bark and kill it. What would Great Elk expect us to do then? Give him the dying corpse of our god?"

Wolf Stone had no answer.

"Even you, my gentle friend," Goodshade said, smiling, "must see that we would protect him. We would fight, and destroy your father and all his tribe."

Wolf Stone sighed heavily. He knew now that his plan was impossible. He wanted to look at Heather, but did not dare. "I find myself always thinking of deception. It is the way I have been taught to think. I am ashamed." Then he looked up at Goodshade. "There is one thing you said that is not possible—you could never defeat Great Elk in war."

"What could he do in a forest with swords against bows?"

"Very little," admitted Wolf Stone. "But you people who think sweetly and honestly would find it hard to believe what my father might do, what he has done to other villages." He shuddered at what he could remember and might prophesy. "Your bramble hedges among the trees would take fire easily in a wind."

Goodshade's eyes narrowed. Blue Wing's bow trembled in his hand.

Wolf Stone looked at them sadly. "Our sun-priest wants to burn your whole forest. Though it gained him nothing, Great Elk might let him." He glanced at the young archer whose eyes smoldered with hatred and fear, and seemed to see himself with this boy's eyes, as Heather must now see him, unworthy of her love! He thought of the lonely, wandering days before him and cried out, "All I wanted was for Heather to live here in peace! I have tried to think of some way. I have failed." He stood up, not daring to glance at her. "I will go now." With what dignity he could, he walked out into the night.

WHEN THE SUN was up and clear of the forest, Goodshade went out to the tree against a gently stirring breeze and assembled those chieftains who remained there as captains of the archers on guard. To the music of bird song, and the laughter of children playing along the shore, and the murmur of the tree, and the happy chatter of the spring, he told what Wolf Stone had revealed—if Great Elk failed to win the tree, his sun-priest would burn the whole forest though it gained him nothing.

The chiefs sat with their heads bowed under the

weight of fear. One of them spoke, then another, nervously, as they considered every way to defend their lives, their villages, and their land from the Sun People. When no answer could be found, they prayed to their god to tell them what to do.

A stronger breeze stirred the leaves, rustling the promise of an answer! Tree Woman was sent for. More clearly than any of the men she understood the words of the tree.

When she arrived, smiling a little in embarrassment, wearing her ceremonial dress of fawn skins mottled like the bark of a sycamore, the breeze had become a wind. At first it blew gustily, then steadily and strongly until the mightly oak was chanting with the voice of the god!

Soon the chanting died away to a murmur, and Tree Woman told what the god had said:

"No war can win the forest from the fury of the sun who is no more a god. No war can quench our fear. Fear cannot save us from war. The archers must return to their villages. The warriors must return to their homes. We must find our greatest treasure and give it to our god. We must be pure of fear. Then the tree will grow and its fruit ripen. These are the words of the god."

With her eyes on the ground, Tree Woman went back to her house, wondering if the chiefs and the archers would dare to be as brave as the tree had asked them to be. She herself was afraid. She was afraid they would take fear with them and it would drift on the air and draw destruction toward them, as the smell of carrion attracts wolves. They must find their greatest treasure and give it to the tree. Then their hearts would be pure again and fearless, and the Sun People would vanish as if they had been only a dream.

What treasure did the tree mean? The Forest People had no treasure except the forest, their cottages, their few animals, their families, and the tree itself.

Heather watched her mother come in and begin to spin thread from a mass of carded wool. "What did the tree say?" she asked wearily.

"He told us to be brave."

Heather agreed that this was good advice. She lay back in a shaft of sunlight slanting down from the smoke-hole and listened to the wind. It hooted under the eaves, whistled in the reeds of the roof, swirled away across the dust outside, and was still. It did not speak to her of her childhood as it used to. It spoke only of Wolf Stone, of how he had stood in the flickering light, how he had gone away without looking at her. She would never see him again. He had gone into emptiness. There was nothing to weep about, nothing to fear, nothing to hope for. There was only a sadness, a wide, lonely sadness.

When the Sun People were gone, she supposed she

would marry Blue Wing as everyone expected her to. She would have children, and love them, and pray to the gods, and grow old. She would smile. Only the spring and the tree would know why she would smile. And Wolf Stone, wherever he was, would know. From beyond her dreams he would watch her. They would speak to each other and smile.

Tree Woman was twisting wool into a thread. Heather had never before seen tears in her mother's eyes. "Why are you crying?" she asked gently. "The tree told us to be brave. Or did he say something else you haven't told me?"

Tree Woman did not answer.

Heather sighed. "If he wants a sacrifice, I have given him everything I hoped for. Let him be satisfied." She went outside and stood for a moment in the sunny wind. Then she walked up the mound. Buzz was there, sitting against the stones, sheltered from the wind, chirping to herself as she twisted tufts of grass into little dolls with daisies for eyes.

"I'm never going to be happy again," she said. "I'm as bad as the Swampwife. I'm going to be just like her. I'm going to live up here all alone and learn how to poison Sun People." She pulled the daisy eyes out of a doll she had made, tore it to pieces, and tossed the shreds of grass into the wind. "I drowned the old woman."

"It wasn't your fault," said Heather.

"It was! I knew what would happen when I buzzed at her!"

"If you hadn't, she might have drowned the other sun-priest."

"I wish she had!" cried Buzz. Then she asked, "Is Wolf Stone going to kill his father?"

"Nobody is going to kill anybody," said Heather patiently.

"He ought to. Then he could be the chief and take his people away. He wants to, doesn't he? So there won't be a war. You want him to take his people away, don't you?"

"Yes."

"Then let him! But don't expect him to take you with him! He never will. He knows you couldn't live the way those wild people do. Even if you were married to him, they'd treat you like a slave. You wouldn't be his only wife either. You couldn't be his wife at all until you killed somebody. Of course"—she glanced at Heather with tears in her eyes—"if he became their chief, maybe he'd change some of the stupid things his people do. Like throwing children into swamps."

"He would, Buzz! He would!" said Heather.

"Then why don't you want him to kill his wicked old father and become the chief?"

Heather was silent. And Buzz cried out, "Somebody's got to!"

"I don't want anyone to kill anyone!"

"Well, what do you want?"

"I don't know! I don't know!" Heather ran down through the hot, dry wind and into the forest. Buzz had stirred hope in her heart, and it hurt like a thorn.

AT DUSK the wind twitched at a leaf, swirled a tuft of grass, and slept.

The forest warriors sat quietly under the tree of Oakwood waiting for Goodshade to send them home. A few had heard Tree Woman tell what the god had said, and the word quickly spread to all of them. They were relieved, eager to return to their villages where they had fields to take care of, animals to feed, and other chores left unfinished when they were called to war. Now there was to be no war. Some were already wiping the paint off their cheeks and chins. Some had unstrung their bows. But still the chieftains sat close to the trunk of the tree in what seemed an endless discussion, weighing each word of the oracle.

Over and over again Goodshade told them to put fear out of their minds. But when they thought of disbanding the archers, leaving the tree undefended, they shook their heads in doubt. A few whose faith was simple became angry at those who doubted, and withdrew from the meeting. Gray Owl wondered if Tree Woman might not have misunderstood the voice of the god. When he was glared into silence, he arose haughtily and stalked away, followed by his troop of archers.

Slowly, trembling from age, Elfstream stood up, his eyes glinting above his white beard. His voice was heard in respectful silence, for he was not only the oldest but the most powerful of all the forest chieftains. "We have been told not to fear," he said, "but how can we not be afraid when we ourselves have caused the danger? Our sacrifices have not pleased the tree. They have been no sacrifice to us, because we have not treasured them."

The chieftains lowered their eyes as the old man continued, "The tree has asked for our greatest treasure. What could that be but one of our lives?"

The archers murmured uneasily, and Goodshade said, "Never before has one of our gods asked for the sacrifice of a life. I do not think that was the meaning in the words of the tree."

"Life is our greatest treasure," said Elfstream stubbornly.

This argument seemed to have no solution. The bowmen began to growl with impatience and so, since the tree had clearly said the guards were to be sent to their homes, Goodshade spoke this order and they returned not too quietly to their villages.

The troubled chiefs still remained to consider the tree's demand. "What is our greatest treasure?" asked Elfstream again and again. And each man thought of his own village, of the pleasant woods he had loved all his life, of his wife and his children. "If each of us gives up these things," said one, "we will be destroyed as surely as if the Sun People burned the forest."

Goodshade at last said quietly, "What our offering must be will be revealed in time. Return now to your homes."

Wearily they drifted away through the twilight, Chief Elfstream still muttering his unpleasant prophecy. The Chief of Oakwood walked slowly toward his village.

As he passed the pool where the animals drank, he paused, then opened the gate of the stockade and let the sheep out to browse, the cows to graze in the forest swales, and the pigs to feed on acorns.

Blue Wing came along the path. Goodshade could see that he was worried. "Speak your doubts, my son. I will try to help you understand them if I can."

"We are all fools!" said Blue Wing bitterly.

"That is true. We know little of what has gone before and can only guess at what is to come. Only the god is wise. He has told us not to fear."

"My father wasn't afraid of anything," muttered the boy. "Not even of wolves. He went everywhere without a weapon. The wolves weren't impressed by his courage. They tore him to bits! Our tree tells us to send the archers away, to leave him undefended. How do we know he doesn't *want* the Sun People to destroy us? They offer better sacrifices than we do. Or perhaps he's testing us to see if we consider him worth defending."

Goodshade sat down on a stone. After a moment he said, "To guard the tree would only point to him. To guard some other tree would be deception. If we show no fear, the Sun People will know we are stronger than they are and will respect us. Not all of them are evil. Wolf Stone, who came to us last night, is not. He is ashamed of his people. He has gone back to face his father with honesty and courage. Wolf Stone may fight our battle for us—because he loves Heather."

In jealous rage, Blue Wing cried out, "He doesn't love her! Not as I do!"

Goodshade sighed. "When the Sun People have gone away, as they will, she will forget him."

"She will never forget him," said Blue Wing. "He will come back for her, and she will go with him!" As he loped away through the dusk he shouted, "I don't intend to unstring *my* bow!"

Goodshade sadly watched him disappear among the trees.

ALL day long Buzz wandered aimlessly in the forest, eating berries and roots when she found them, watching the wind surge through the treetops or, at intervals when the wind was still, listening to the happy singing of the innocent birds.

When night fell, she went out to the mound and crawled into the little cave under the boulders. There, as she listened to the silence she wondered, now that Wolf Stone had saved Heather's life, if he would take her away with him. The child felt terribly alone and whispered over and over how sorry she was she had buzzed at the poor, lonely old woman.

Suddenly Buzz held her breath. Outside the cave she heard a cautious footstep. There, in the white glare of moonlight, she saw two big, ugly, dirty feet. Backing away, she bumped her head and cried out. Before she knew what was happening, she was dragged by the hair into the white night and hurled roughly into the shadow of the stones.

Eagle looked closely at the frightened child and snarled, "Those marks on your forehead prove you are one of us. What are you doing here?"

"I live here," said Buzz faintly.

"Are you a slave of the Forest People?"

She nodded.

With his big clumsy hand he stroked her hair. In terror she almost buzzed at him. He drew his hand away and asked, "Do you like the Forest People?"

"Yes."

"So do I." He gazed down at the small dark houses among the trees. "I would rather live here as a slave than be a captain of the Sun People."

"So would I," said Buzz. "The Forest People never sacrifice people, and they don't like fighting." Ugly as Eagle was, with his long, thin nose like a bird's beak, she was no longer afraid of him.

He glanced about cautiously and whispered, "Do you

know why I came here? To warn the Forest People that Great Elk is planning to attack them."

"We know it," said Buzz.

Eagle was surprised. "I don't see anyone ready to defend himself. Where are the bowmen I've heard about?"

Buzz didn't answer.

"Perhaps I shouldn't ask." He looked down at the ground. "If they knew what I know, they'd know there's only one way to keep Great Elk from coming here and killing everybody he doesn't make a slave." He looked into her wide, scared eyes. "One little girl like you could do more than a whole army to keep Great Elk from doing what he plans to do. I shouldn't tell my secret plan to a person I don't know. You might give me away to the Sun People, and they'd kill me."

"I never would!" whispered Buzz.

"You could help me make them go away forever if you cared to."

"How?" asked the child eagerly. "Tell me!"

"First, you'd have to promise never to tell anyone you've talked to me."

"I never will, ever! I promise!" She touched the blue dots above her eyebrows. "Tell me, what is your secret plan?"

"All you have to do is bring me certain things I need."

"What do you need?"

"A sharp flint ax."

"That's easy. There are hundreds in a pool I know of. What else?"

"A bow and a few arrows."

Buzz hesitated. "What do you want them for?"

"To do something everybody in our tribe wants done but is afraid to do."

"What?"

"To kill someone who wants to burn this whole forest."

"Great Elk?"

"Yes."

The way Eagle said this was like a snake hissing, and Buzz was afraid again. "If you have to kill somebody, why do you need a stone ax and a bow and arrow? Why don't you stick him with a sword?"

"Because bronze won't touch him. Great Elk holds a spell over bronze. Poison would be a good way, but his slave can smell every poison we know of. Of course, if I could find some leaves that taste and smell as sweet as clover . . ."

Buzz knew the Swampwife had leaves that smelled like clover. The dry black leaves she burned in her fire. The same ones she poisoned Fang and his puppies with. The child shuddered. "I don't want you to kill the old man!"

"Wouldn't that be better than letting him burn the forest?"

"Yes." She stood up, trembling. "I'll get you the things you want. Shall I bring them here?"

"No." He pointed toward the forest to a tree with one dead white branch in the top of it. "Over there, by that tree."

Buzz ran down the mound, across the meadow, and into the birch grove.

Eagle smiled a twisted smile and went stumbling down the other side of the mound and into the forest. His blundering through the bushes was noisy, which was why no one had caught him wandering about until he found the tree he wanted. Everyone knew no enemy would be so noisy. They thought he was just a browsing cow.

THE FOREST had always before spoken to Heather and she had understood the voices of insects, the chattering of birds, and the murmuring of leaves. She still heard these summer voices, but they were speaking to each other, not to her. The forest did not care to hear about Wolf Stone. He was gone. He might come back, and he might not. It was foolish to think any more about him.

A butterfly flitted by on its painted wings, and Heather thought only of how soon it would die. Leaves above her seemed to be turning brittle while they were still green.

Everything on the earth seemed to be busily dying. And then silence spoke to her. It told her how wrong it was to hope, or to be afraid. She was ashamed. She had been hoping, but fearing too, that Wolf Stone would kill his father. Now she was angry at Buzz for making her hope and fear. Then she felt how wicked it was to be angry at the child, who was hurt and sad because of what she had done to the Swampwife. Heather sighed. No wonder the voices of the forest would not speak to her!

She sat down on the cool soft moss and stroked it as if it were a small woolly puppy. One of Fang's puppies. Now they were dead. But Wolf Stone was alive. He loved her. He would always love her as she would always love him. Always.

Suddenly she leaped up. Now she knew what the silence had been trying to tell her! She would forget that she had ever met Wolf Stone in this dying world! They had known each other long before they met. Even if he never came back, they would always be together in that world where nothing ever dies! She listened to the voices of the forest and once more understood them. One of the happiest of these was the voice of the spring. She went there and drank the cool refreshing water. It was only water pouring out of clean hard rock, making a pleasant sound as it splashed into the pool. It was not a god any more, but just a spring being a spring. To Heather this seemed more wonderful than if it were a god. Everything was a god! "We are, we are, we are," sang all the natural voices of the earth, and she echoed them:

"I am too. And so is Wolf Stone!"

Among the sounds of the forest she also heard the sound of someone trying to walk quietly not far away among the trees. Even before she saw him she knew that it was Blue Wing.

She watched him pouncing like a bear along the edge of the forest, muttering and grunting to himself. He was hiding arrows so that he would seem unarmed and then, when he wanted them again, he could quickly find them. Under the moss at the base of a tree he hid an arrow and went on to another tree where he hid another arrow, his last, and his taut-strung bow. For a moment he stood looking out across the clearing that led on one side up the sandy hills and on the other to the long wood. Heather could almost hear him thinking that if Wolf Stone came back either way, he would have to cross this open space.

When Heather stepped up to Blue Wing, he started guiltily and flapped his empty hands exactly as if they were paws. He tried so hard to look innocent that she laughed and said, "If he does come back, I don't think he will come this way. He will come riding a horse, and in armor, with a horsetail plume on his helmet, and with warriors in armor but without weapons. He will come back as the son of a chieftain." Blue Wing's face darkened. And she added, "If he ever comes back in this world." She turned and scuffed up an arrow and the bow hidden under the moss.

Blue Wing mumbled, "I wonder how those got there."

Heather's laughter rang out in the stillness, and Blue Wing's snub-nosed face was puzzled. "You don't seem to care if he comes back or not."

"Of course, I care. But if he doesn't, I won't die. I won't even cry." She held out the bow to him. He took it hesitantly and, as she watched him, quickly unstrung it. She handed him the arrow. He broke it across his knee, and stood holding the two parts of it, looking in dismay at what he had done. Suddenly in a rage he threw the broken arrow onto the ground and in a rage seized her by the arms. "You made me do that! And now you're smiling!" He shook her roughly and shouted, "Why are you smiling?"

She still smiled into his frightened, angry eyes and said, "Because I want you to sing to me the way you used to, and tell me to stop being a child."

"I won't!" he said sullenly. "I know you love Wolf Stone!" He looked at her as if he had never seen her before. "You do, don't you?"

"Yes."

In rage and terror and confusion, he turned and ran into the forest.

Heather listened until she could no longer hear him. Then she listened again. Someone was watching her and had been watching her and Blue Wing. She guessed it was Buzz, and called. There was no answer.

Outside the zigzag gate she met her father and Littleman. It was they who had been watching her. She smiled at them and said, "Blue Wing is not afraid of Wolf Stone any more. He's afraid of me." She laughed lightly and went on toward her house.

Goodshade and Littleman watched her go. They said nothing. They moved on into the forest to find Blue Wing.

Heather was right. Buzz had also been watching her, but had good reason not to answer. Near the bee tree the child met Eagle and gave him the things he had asked for: Chief Goodshade's bow and a quiver fat with arrows, a yellowed but still hafted flint ax she had stolen from the spring, and a small brown nutshell sealed with beeswax she had found among the Swampwife's herbs. Buzz knew the shell was filled with a powder made from the black leaves that had killed Fang and his puppies. It smelled sweetly of clover.

Eagle was pleased. He put the wax-covered shell carefully in his tunic and stuck the ax into his belt. With satisfaction he fitted an arrow to the string of the bow and aimed it at the trunk of the tree. He did not shoot.

The arrow fell out of his clumsy fingers. Behind him he heard a snort of derision.

Buzz vanished among the underbrush as Blue Wing went up to Eagle and said angrily, "Those are Goodshade's weapons!"

"They're mine now," snarled Eagle.

"You've never held a bow before," said the forest boy with contempt.

"I intend to find the best bowman in the world to use it."

"Who would that be? Wolf Stone?"

Eagle spat. "Not that pigeon!"

"Who?" asked Blue Wing again.

"Some pig-faced forest archer who knows he could, if he cared to, defeat Great Elk's whole army with one arrow."

Blue Wing flushed and asked, "Are you the enemy of your own people?"

Eagle's eyes were as hard with hate as a hawk's. "My only enemy is Great Elk."

"Why do you hate him?"

"Because he wants to burn this forest."

"Why do you care if he does?"

Eagle looked up at the tall curved branch of the tree under which they stood. "Because I want to make a ship of this tree."

"You think this is the tree of power?"

Eagle sneered. "I know it's not. I've seen that one too. It has too many branches."

Blue Wing was silent for a moment. Then he asked, "How could one arrow defeat Great Elk?"

"By killing him," said Eagle bluntly. "Wolf Stone would then be chieftain and would do what his brothers tell him to do, which is what I tell them to do!"

"What would happen," asked Blue Wing slowly, "if by some accident, while I was teaching your warriors to use that bow, an arrow happened to kill Great Elk?"

"You would have nothing to fear."

"It is said that your sun-priest is more powerful than your chief, and is the one who wants to burn our forest."

Eagle picked his teeth with a thorn and again spat. "When Great Elk dies, Troll Tamer will die with him because of a curse between them. If he doesn't . . . there might be a second accident." He handed Blue Wing the bow and the quiver full of arrows.

"I think," said the forest boy, "that Wolf Stone is not so timid as you believe."

Eagle shrugged. "Who knows, there might be a third small accident."

Blue Wing bounced a little on the soles of his feet. "Who then would be chief of your tribe? You?"

Eagle's eyes blinked beside his beak of a nose, and

his wide mouth spread out in a twisted smile. He drew in his breath sharply. He was surprised that he had never before thought of this possibility. The veins on his temples began to throb, and he said, "Yes. I would become the chief. There would be no war. I would build my ship without interference, and leave your people in peace. You would be known to everyone as the man who saved this forest from being burned and your people from destruction by war."

With a quick hot glare back toward the meadow where he had recently left Heather, Blue Wing glanced at Eagle and nodded. Together they marched away into the long wood.

Goodshade and Littleman watched them go. And Buzz, who had crept out of the bramble hedge, watched them go.

To Goodshade, Littleman said, "Blue Wing has gone to teach the Sun People how to destroy us." The chief shook his head as if he could not believe what he had seen.

Buzz was ashamed and afraid. "I heard what they said. That ugly man is going to make Blue Wing kill Wolf Stone."

After a moment Littleman said, "I would go across the heath to warn them, but I move too slowly." He looked at Buzz.

Her lips trembled, but she said, "I will go. I'm

scared, but I'll go." She ran across the meadow, over the sandy hills, and on into the glaring, sun-dazzled, desolate heath toward the camp of the Sun People.

Heather knew nothing of all this. She sat under the cooking shelter with Tree Woman, telling how the silence in the forest had taught her not to hope. Then she would not be afraid, not even of loneliness if she never saw Wolf Stone again in this world.

WOLF STONE's long walk back to his camp seemed endless as he stumbled through darkness. But when the sun arose and spread its golden warmth over the earth, he stood in the emptiness of the heath, in the emptiness of light, until he knew that he had been living for years in darkness, blinded by the stone-blind eyes of Troll Tamer.

He remembered when he was a boy in a wide, windy land where herds of game roamed through tall grass, where flocks of birds settled and twittered all night in the few trees that grew there, where fish could be caught among the rocks in a stream. In those days the Sun People had been happy.

Great Elk had been a slender young man who loved the sun dancing in the sky. He had taught his youngest son to make swords and bracelets of bronze. Once he gave a sword away to a wild chieftain from the mountains who then tried to kill him with it. For a while he made war only on those mountain people. But as he pursued them farther and farther, he made new enemies of tribes whose lands he crossed, whose cattle he stole to feed his warriors, and soon he was satisfied by nothing except wandering and war.

This life had been exciting to Wolf Stone until his father grew tired of being the sun-priest to his people and gave this power to a man who saw only visions but nothing of this world. Year by year Troll Tamer had taken more of the sun's power to himself, as Great Elk concerned himself only with the barbaric, lusty pleasures of war. Now, both men were bound by hatred in a blood curse, and the once happy Sun People were more afraid of their own leaders than of any enemy. Even the captains had begun to hate their father as much as they hated Troll Tamer. It seemed to Wolf Stone that his tribe was about to destroy itself.

But that morning, as the sun spoke to him in the stillness of the heath, he knew at last what he had to do.

When he stepped into his father's tent, Great Elk watched him shrewdly and said, "You have the look of a man who has just won a battle."

The boy shook his head. "Not yet." He smiled with affection at the untidy, grizzle-bearded old chieftain, knowing how easily he might arouse his unpredictable anger.

Great Elk watched him closely. "I guessed you were out on some adventure of your own."

Wolf Stone placed his hand on the old man's mottled, slightly tremulous hand and said, "Someday, I want to be the leader of your people. When that time comes I want to be as brave as you." He took a deep breath and said bluntly, "I don't want to go about the world in a ship that can never be sunk! In any ship at all!"

Great Elk looked at his son with astonishment. "Why haven't you told me this before?"

"Because your search for the tree has given you pleasure."

The chief coughed and rumbled and then laughed more heartily than he had for years. "The search for the tree has given me pleasure. But now, when we find it, I will let Eagle do what he wants with it. Troll Tamer can burn it if he wishes. If you prefer the earth and its mountains and grasslands, then stick to the earth, my son. To tell you the truth, I don't care much for the sea myself."

"Then why has this dream of a ship been so important to you?"

Great Elk smiled. "That is all it has been—a dream, a longing for the sun to take me aboard his golden ship. I have lived my life. Now I would be glad to join your mother. My sorrow is to see her beyond the edge of darkness, to call to her and not be heard."

"That I understand," said Wolf Stone, "since I too love a girl I may never see again. A girl of the forest. She loves me, but her people do not."

Great Elk snorted, "If taking her calls for a war, I'll put you in command of my whole army!"

The boy stood up and walked across the tent. "She hates war."

"Then forget her!"

"Can you forget my mother?"

The chief banged the arm of his chair with his cup and shouted, "All right, tell me what you want me to do and we'll do it! What holds you back?"

"The tree of power."

"Forget the tree!"

"It grows in her village. Her people know you want to make a ship of it."

"No longer!"

"They know Troll Tamer wants to burn it, to burn the whole forest and all the people in it."

Great Elk's cheeks flushed as he growled, "The captains will rid us of Troll Tamer." He grumbled to himself for a moment and then said, "I will make Longfire head priest in his place."

Wolf Stone watched his father closely. "Did Longfire bring you a present from me?"

"What kind of present?" Before the boy could reply, Great Elk shouted, "I'm not afraid of Troll Tamer! I don't believe in his curse. But even if it is true—" He broke off his thought and laughed. "Tell me about your girl. And her people."

Slowly Wolf Stone said, "Her name is Heather. Her father is Goodshade. He is the chief of a people as shy as deer. They are afraid of anything beautiful or strange." The boy stood gazing out through the rolled-up side of the tent at the cattle grazing beside the lake. "They are slaves of their forest as we are slaves of our animals."

Great Elk sipped his ale, remembering the green land where he had lived as a young man, where winter and summer there was grass for his cattle and he had no reason to wander.

Wolf Stone was thinking of the vision that had come to him in the early sunshine. "Some day," he said, "there may be a tribe freer than either of us, loving life as we do, as brave as we are, but more gentle, more just. Some day the Forest People and the Sun People may be one tribe under one god who is a tree whose fruit and seed is the sun. This greater tribe may remember you as their ancestor."

Great Elk sighed, "I would like to be remembered." Then gruffly he pointed across the tent to a chest where he kept his treasure. "In there is the first thing I ever made of bronze. Your mother wore it all her life. Give it to your forest girl."

In the chest Wolf Stone found a carved bronze disk. It was the work of a young man before he had become expert in his craft. To Wolf Stone it was beautiful. He said, "The children of my children will remember the brave man who made this."

Great Elk was content.

At last Great Elk had given the command for the captains to destroy Troll Tamer. He had said he didn't believe in the curse, but if it were true, he would be glad to go to the land of the sun. Still, it was easy to see how deeply he feared death, how unsure that there was a land of the sun to which he might go. His faith in the god had long ago been darkened by Troll Tamer's cruel and fanatical worship.

The old chief's confused hope and dread saddened Wolf Stone who believed in his god as simply as when he was a child. He had no doubt at all about the land we all come from and return to after this life. As he walked toward the tent of the captains, he knew that what he had to do was the sun's command, and that the strength he felt was not his own but the sun's.

A deep voice stopped suddenly as he stepped into the tent shared by eight of his brothers, those chosen warriors who were called the captains. Longfire, who sat with them, was in armor, his sword across his knees.

Wolf Stone had not heard what they were discussing, but he guessed it was not favorable to him. He sat down in their circle next to Oxenstar and looked at each of them in turn. A slight tightness in a smile, or a drifting of eyes told him they no longer felt that Great Elk's choice of a successor suited them.

"Yesterday," said Wolf Stone, "Oxenstar asked me if I would succeed my father. I will. It is his wish."

"We do not want a chief who defends Troll Tamer," said Badger bluntly.

"Troll Tamer must die," said Wolf Stone.

"When?"

"Today."

"Does Great Elk agree to this?"

"It is his command."

All except Longfire took in a breath of relief.

Badger was watching Wolf Stone. "If Great Elk isn't afraid of Troll Tamer's curse, why hasn't he got rid of him long ago?"

Wolf Stone did not reply. He looked at Longfire,

whose face was a mask, and asked, "Where is the amber I sent as a present to my father?"

Longfire pointed up to the breastplate which hung on a thong stretched across the tent.

Oxenstar turned angrily to the sun-priest. "You said *you* had found it! That it was a present to me!"

Longfire rumbled guiltily, "I couldn't believe you would accept Wolf Stone as your chief."

Badger laughed shortly. "He is not our choice, but our father's."

The captains had not noticed the change in Wolf Stone. But as Longfire stared at the boy he was awed by his quiet assurance and knew that such power came only from the sun. "I will never again be so stupid," muttered the priest.

"If I had the authority," said Wolf Stone, "I would ask you to prove yourself worthy to take Troll Tamer's place by destroying him."

Sweat broke out on Longfire's face. "I've tried to. I told no one. But he knew. He knows now what we are saying!"

Wolf Stone stood up, took down the amber, and tossed it to the sun-priest. "Take this to Great Elk. He will tell you what to do."

Longfire's powerful hands shook as he hung the amber breastplate over his shoulder, sheathed his sword, loosened the dagger at his belt and put on his white robe.

As he went out, all the captains felt his terror. And all of them looked at Wolf Stone as he said, "If I had the authority, I would send you out among your men to tell them, when the lurs sound, not to go to the dancing field, but to stay close to the tent of Great Elk."

The captains stood up, silent, and strapped on their sword belts. Badger hesitated a moment, with a wry smile of admiration for his youngest brother. When Oxenstar moved to go, Wolf Stone said, "Wait!" The word was quietly spoken, but it was a command.

Oxenstar flushed and waited, and Wolf Stone said, "Until the sun told me what I must do, it was not my ambition to become the chief. I'd rather stay in the forest with a girl I love. But I can't. Our tribe is a threat to hers. Neither can I bring her to live in this tribe as it is, poisoned by hatred and fear." Oxenstar listened without expression, and Wolf Stone continued. "Our god is the greatest above all gods. The god of the Forest People is only a tree, with roots in the earth, who must someday die as we do. But there is wisdom in such a great plant that has lived longer than any person. He speaks to his people, and they hear him. Great Elk no longer wants to destroy that tree. It is his dream, as it is mine, to see the Forest People and the Sun People become one tribe. If he must die to see this done, afraid of death as he is, he is ready to die. He has asked us to free him and our people and the sorrowing sun from Troll Tamer."

After a moment, Oxenstar put his arm across Wolf Stone's shoulder, and they went out together toward the tent of their father.

On their way across the camp, they watched the tall shining sun-disk tip slowly down behind the tents and disappear. They followed an excited crowd and saw that slaves had lashed ropes to the rim of the golden disk and were pulling it over. People had gathered about it, women shrieking at children who strayed too close, sun-priests shouting to clear a way for slaves who were grunting and cursing as they tugged at ropes, whips snapping against their sweating backs.

A girl warrior, a member of the Doves, swaggered by, pretending—as was usual with the Doves—to be indifferent to any excitement not of their own making.

Oxenstar called to her, "What's happening?"

She looked at him coolly. Then she said to Wolf Stone, "Troll Tamer has decided the sun needs a new plating of gold. Today there will be no dancing."

The boys exchanged a glance. The girl noticed it and asked, "Could this have anything to do with something you had planned?"

"It has nothing to do with us!" said Oxenstar.

Wolf Stone watched the girl's eyes and asked, "Are you Doves ready to dance for Great Elk if he needs entertainment?"

"We are ready," she said. Saluting Wolf Stone with

her sword, she made a face at Oxenstar and asked, "Who scratched your face this time, Captain?" She spun her blade in the air, sheathed it, and strolled away.

"I don't think it's safe to let those stupid girls know our plans," muttered Oxenstar.

"Why not? Troll Tamer knows them."

"How could he!"

"Our slaves are his spies."

Slowly, between the tents, came a procession of sun-priests, armed under their robes.

Circling the wagons, the boys hurried toward Great Elk's tent.

Not everyone had been drawn to the excitement around the sun-disk. A few warriors were drifting toward the lake. On the grass in sight of the chief's tent others sprawled idly in the sun, gambling with bone sticks or seeming to be asleep. The Doves sat under a small tree, polishing their armor.

Behind Great Elk's tent with its elk skulls on tall poles, Wolf Stone suddenly gripped his brother's arm. They had almost tripped over the body of a sun-priest. They heaved him over. It was Longfire. His robe was stained with blood. His own dagger still pierced his breast.

Oxenstar's scarred face went white. "Troll Tamer knows what Longfire intended, and knows now what we intend."

"He also knows," said Wolf Stone grimly, "that the sun is no longer his slave." He drew the amber out from under Longfire's robe.

Great Elk sat in the shade of his awning, his cup in his hand, a comfortable smile on his face.

Wolf Stone stepped before him and held out the present of amber. It was a greater treasure than any golden cup.

The chief was as delighted as a child. "Where did you find this?" he asked.

"Floating on a marsh. I sent it to you in Longfire's hands. Now Longfire is dead."

Great Elk was startled. Then he growled his indifference.

Wolf Stone helped him put the breastplate over his head. It covered his broad chest with polished knobs of amber that caught and pooled the light. The old man caressed the almost weightless nuggets of sea-gold, and murmured, "I would like to take this with me when I go."

The sun-priests were approaching, led by Troll Tamer.

Wolf Stone spoke in a low voice. "If this means a battle, it may be the best way."

Great Elk listened to the slow shuffling march of the priests and gripped the arms of his chair.

The two men who guided Troll Tamer with a touch

on his elbows might have been Knife and Longfire. Their faces were stone masks. They stopped just under the shadow of the awning and stepped back, and Troll Tamer fixed his sightless eyes on Great Elk.

"There will be no dancing today," he said in his soft voice. "Instead, we will have games. The lurs will sound for a tournament of arms. The Forest People will be watching us. They will soon lose their caution and we will turn on them and take their tree."

"Have you found the tree?" asked Great Elk pleasantly.

Before Troll Tamer could reply, Eagle slouched forward and said, "I have found it and have brought a hostage to trade for it." He nudged before him a snubnosed young man who carried over his shoulder a quiver full of arrows and an unstrung bow. "This boy is Blue Wing. He is the best archer in his village, and the best maker of arrow points. In exchange for his life the Forest People will give us the tree. They do not value it as you thought. Their important god is a spring. There will be no need to fight for the tree."

"I am no longer interested in the tree," Great Elk said with a smile.

Eagle opened his wide mouth and in amazement snapped it shut.

Great Elk laughed. "You frightened me out of all interest in the tree when you offered me my choice of how to die. You scared out of me all desire to build a ship, any ship at all, or to fight against your brother. You should be pleased because now, when you take back your treasure, you won't have to share it with me. I will see that you are given leather shoes for your march against your brother as an army of one."

"I will sail against him in a ship!" snarled Eagle. "I will destroy my brother and take back my treasure which is greater than any you have ever seen!" His eyes roamed wildly about. Everywhere they met hostility, and he pounded his clumsy fists on his chest and shouted, "I am the only one of you who knows how to build a ship!"

"I told you I am no longer interested in ships," said Great Elk coldly.

"Not even if it is cut from the tree of power?" asked Eagle with a sly glance toward Troll Tamer.

"Least of all am I interested in that wise old god of the Forest People. He is to be honored with the same respect as our own god! This is my command!" Great Elk's eyes flicked over Eagle as if dismissing him from existence, and Eagle, choking and purple with rage, pushed himself awkwardly through the crowd and stumbled away among the tents and the wagons.

As Great Elk roared with laughter, Troll Tamer lifted his sightless eyes to the sun and cried out in a shrill voice, "The tree will be burned! And all those who worship it!"

"It will not be burned," said the chief mildly. "Or made into a ship." He was amused to see how he had startled and confused both Troll Tamer and Eagle. He chuckled and held out his hand toward the boy from the forest. "Let me see your weapons."

Blue Wing handed him one barbed shaft and the bow.

Great Elk examined both carefully. Then he smiled and said to Blue Wing, "After our games you will be returned to your village. You will tell your chief he has nothing to fear from me. His god will not be harmed. What is your chief's name?"

"Goodshade."

"You will tell Chief Goodshade that I want only his friendship."

Blue Wing nodded. Great Elk returned to him the bow and the arrow, saying quietly to Badger, "We will start our tournament with this forest boy teaching us how to shoot a bow."

Blue Wing stepped back, humble, and a little confused. He could not understand why this barbaric old chieftain suddenly wanted the friendship of the Forest People. It must be true, since he had defied his own people in saying so. And then he noticed for the first time, Wolf Stone, proud, slender, and assured standing beside his father. It was suddenly clear to Blue Wing that Great Elk wanted his son to marry Heather! A storm of hatred whirled through his mind, leaving him smoldering more feverishly than ever with jealousy.

"Sound the lurs!" shouted Badger.

Two tall, curved bronze trumpets arose above the heads of the crowd and sounded a deep-voiced, mysterious hooting that seemed to melt Blue Wing's blood and bones! Great Elk gave a command for everyone to assemble for an afternoon of games to honor the sacred tree of the Forest People, and this word was shouted from voice to voice through the camp.

Troll Tamer stood motionless, silent, his stone-blind eyes lifted to the sun. Only his long thin fingers twitched slightly.

A GUST of dusty wind blew through the cloudless heat as, on opposite sides of the field, two shelters were set up, one for Great Elk and one for Troll Tamer.

With a clatter of arms and armor, the snorting of mounts and the pawing and pounding of hoofs, the captains assembled their troops around the margin of the field. They were divided into two teams, the Horsedancers wearing red horsehair plumes, the Night Wolves wearing black.

Greak Elk's chair was moved to his shelter beside the field. About him sat those men of his council who were not in the games. A skin full of ale hung in the shade, and his slave was there to keep his cup filled. He was happy and excited.

At one side, Blue Wing was stringing his bow.

The armed and armored sun-priests made no move to take part in the tournament. The sword dance they had planned was not announced. They ranged themselves stiffly in two rows behind Troll Tamer as they did at the dancing ceremony.

Wolf Stone stood apart from the crowd where he could see both the priests and his loyal troops of captains and Doves. Near Great Elk's pavilion, Oxenstar and Badger watched Wolf Stone for a signal if the priests or the slaves huddled about Troll Tamer's pavilion should make a threatening move.

A straw target was placed at one end of the field, the lurs sounded, and everyone became quiet as the first event was announced: a display of archery by a warrior from the forest!

Blue Wing ambled out into the field. At a mark scratched in the dust, he stuck two arrows into the ground. A third he fitted to the string, drew the feathers to his cheek, and let it fly. Before it found the target, a second was in the air, and a third! All struck the heart of the target. A cheer went up, a short cheer followed by an awed silence.

The priests showed no response to Blue Wing's skill.

Wolf Stone was watching them cautiously when a little girl stepped in front of him and stood silently gazing at him. With a start, he realized that the child was Heather's slave! She was hot and tired and disheveled.

"Why are you here?" he asked in a low voice.

"To warn you that Blue Wing loves Heather and is jealous. He came here to kill you."

Again the lurs brayed. Buzz shut her ears and trembled at the sound. Wolf Stone glanced at the young forest archer standing in the field, carefully removing the feathers from an arrow. Blue Wing wet the sinew in his mouth, and bound the feathers on again just behind the stone point. Then he stood for a moment to feel the flow of the wind.

Wolf Stone glanced at Buzz and asked, "Does Heather love this boy?"

"No!" said the child quickly. "She loves you! If you asked her to, she would go with you anywhere!"

A deep warmth filled Wolf Stone. He laughed softly.

"She would come to you," said Buzz, "but it would be nicer if you would come for her and ask her father, who would let her go because he likes you and knows you love each other."

Smiling, Wolf Stone said, "Tell Heather I will come for her, soon." His face sobered as Blue Wing shot his stripped arrow up into a sudden gust. All eyes followed the shaft as it rose, curved back, and sped down. Blue

Wing, standing where he had shot, caught it out of the air.

Again there were cheers.

"When will you come for her?" asked Buzz.

"Soon," said Wolf Stone. He touched the child's head gently. "Wait here. I will have one of my captains take you back to tell her what I have said."

Great Elk was as delighted by Blue Wing's skill as if the boy had been one of his own sons. He cheered and coughed from the dust and held out his empty cup to be filled. He shouted for his slave. Still holding his cup, he called hoarsely to Badger to award Blue Wing a bronze sword as a trophy. In his excitement, Great Elk did not notice who filled his cup. All at once he saw that it had been filled. As he raised it once more, he thought of another game for Blue Wing to play before the tournament between the Horse-dancers and the Night Wolves began. Oxenstar went out to arrange it.

Great Elk's instructions did not please Blue Wing, although he had to accept them. A circle ten paces across was marked in the dust around him. Standing in its center, with a quiver full of arrows, he was to battle the girl warriors, the Doves, mounted and armed with shields and swords. If any one of the girls rode inside the circle, she was to cast away her shield, and Blue Wing was ordered to aim to kill! If he did not, and wavered, the Doves would discard their shields and close in on him and carve him to bits!

Badger, who sat on his horse beside Great Elk's pavilion, was so absorbed in the shouted instructions that he did not notice Wolf Stone trying to catch his attention.

Suddenly a shrill, savage cry went up as the Doves surrounded Blue Wing, riding wildly, leaping off their ponies on one side then the other, sitting backward, shrieking taunts, flaunting swords and shields, their ponies pounding up a blinding screen of dust.

Blue Wing turned with their dizzy circling, an arrow ready, but could find no one target. All at once, the Doves lifted their swords and threw them spinning through the air! They struck, points in the ground, enclosing him in a narrow circle of quivering blades.

A roar of laughter went up. Great Elk shouted his admiration for the skill of the Doves, and coughed happily until he could scarcely see.

Now without weapons, the girls continued to ride in a circle around Blue Wing, who was so angry he shot swiftly, arrow after arrow! Not one struck even a horse, so skillfully the Doves dodged and shifted, although several shafts were deflected from shields into the crowd where children and slaves tussled to claim them.

At last Blue Wing had spent all his arrows. He threw down his bow angrily in defeat. Swiftly the girls rode up to him. Wheeling, each seized her own sword and cantered quietly off the field.

During the combat there had been great surges of delighted shouting, but now a strange disturbed silence fell over Troll Tamer's pavilion. At the dusty peak of excitement, no one had noticed what had happened. But now, when the game was over, Troll Tamer's priests discovered that he had been pierced to the heart by an arrow and was stone dead.

Soon two sun-priests came marching across the field toward Great Elk's shelter. A strained silence settled over the crowd. Slaves slunk away to their quarters. Wolf Stone moved quickly and stood beside his father.

The marching priests, their faces like stone masks, stepped before Great Elk, and one of them said, "Troll Tamer is dead."

The old chief moved his lips to speak, but he could not. With fear in his eyes he looked at Wolf Stone, who gripped his shoulder firmly, with affection.

Holding his heavy gold cup with two hands to keep it from trembling, Great Elk drank. His eyes looked out, startled, toward the field where Troll Tamer's body was being borne away. His hand groped for Wolf Stone's. He tried to smile, to speak. The cup slipped from his numb fingers and rolled away. Then he sighed, as if deeply content, and died.

Unnoticed, Eagle lazily picked up Great Elk's gold cup, dropped it into a leather sack, and strolled away.

Buzz could see only a little of this from where she stood. But she soon knew that Wolf Stone's father had died. And that Eagle had poisoned him with the poison in the nutshell she had given him. Her eyes filled with tears, and a cold mist of shame closed about her heart. All around her people were saying that Blue Wing wasn't to blame. Great Elk had died because of a curse. But Buzz knew better. It had to happen. She had wanted it to happen. But it was an awful thing to know that she had helped it to happen.

Wolf Stone at last came walking toward her. His face was calm but his eyes were sad. Hardly daring to look at him she asked, "Are you the chief now?"

He nodded. Then he looked past her, past the lake, toward the village of Oakwood. It was a long way across the heath, but he could see people standing on the sandy hills. He wondered if one of them was Heather. At the thought of her, his face softened. From his tunic he drew a round object wrapped in leather. He unfolded the leather and looked at a beautiful bronze sun-disk. Buzz knew that he was breathing into it a message for Heather. At that moment Badger walked his horse up, and Wolf Stone said to Buzz, "My brother will take you home. Tell Heather that as soon as my father is buried I will come for her." He handed the leather-wrapped bronze disk to Badger and lifted the child up behind the saddle.

As the horse snorted and pranced, Buzz looked out fearfully toward the field. It was empty now except for Blue Wing who was ambling about looking for an unbroken arrow.

Wolf Stone noticed her worried look, and as the horse galloped away, he remembered her warning. To Oxen-star he said, "Have the forest boy tied up and guarded. He came here to kill me."

THE MORNING after the Swampwife was drowned, children in all parts of the forest sensed that something dangerous had happened, and that something even more mysterious and exciting was still to happen. None of them said anything to their parents about what they felt. It was the kind of thing most older people had forgotten how to feel. But all through the woods, children went flitting along secret paths to find out if any of their playmates knew what had happened. This tingling hint of danger was not at all like the disturbance a few days ago when their fathers had painted their cheeks and chins red and slipped away in the night leaving them with men's chores to do. That danger had come to nothing. But in some way the children knew that this mystery had to do with one of their own.

It was two days before they found out that little Buzz who lived in Oakwood had buzzed an old witch to death in a swamp. Soon they began to flit out of the forest to stand gazing at the swamp where the old woman had sunk under the mud. Creeping cautiously into the hut of reeds, they sniffed the smells of dried herbs. They discovered treasure under the firestone and gazed at bronze and gold and amber, but did not dare touch any of those beautiful and evil things made by the Sun People.

They tried to find Buzz to hear just how she had buzzed the old witch to death, but no one in Oakwood had seen her all day.

When the sound of the lurs came drifting faintly on waves of wind, the children were the first to peek out over the crests of the sandy hills, happily fascinated with terror as clouds of dust arose above the camp of the Sun People.

Heather came out into the sunlight and sat alone, openly on the highest hill, not far from her father who also sat alone. The children watched them and whispered together. They knew the sun-god had come to Heather in the shape of a young man who wanted to take her away with him into the sky. But her father had sent the sun away to the camp of the Sun People, and the dust over there was probably caused by their dancing.

Even Chief Goodshade knew it was not a war dance. He was sad because his daughter had fallen in love with the sun, but he was not afraid. Heather wasn't either sad or afraid. She sat as still as a tree, listening to the lurs, watching the cloud of dust and smiling. One of the children asked her if dancing made the dust and she said, "I think so. I think the Sun People are choosing a new chieftain."

"Buzz would know," said the little girl. "Buzz knows everything. But we can't find her. Maybe she's over there watching."

Heather didn't say, and so the little girl ran back to the other children and whispered that Buzz had gone over to the camp of the Sun People. They shivered happily, wondering what Buzz could tell them when she came back.

Without glancing at his daughter, Goodshade said, "It is true, Buzz is there. She went to warn Wolf Stone that Blue Wing intends to kill him."

Heather's face became very pale.

Littleman came hobbling slowly up the hill and said something to Goodshade, who stood up and went back to the village. Littleman sat down wearily on the sand. He wanted to speak to Heather. But she did not seem to notice him.

Now and then a few people, and then a few more, came up and sat on the hills or stood in small groups watching the faraway cloud of dust. When the lurs hooted they did not seem to enjoy the mysterious sound as the children did.

Soon Goodshade came back, and with him was old, white-bearded Chief Elfstream and his archers. Their faces were not painted red, but their bows were strung and their quivers full.

Suddenly everyone was silent. The distant cloud of dust began to drift away. Soon, all that anyone could see under it was a bare field. No sound at all came from the camp. Nothing moved except the shimmering heat. And one wagon. Stirring up its own plume of dust, it drove slowly over the heath toward the long wood. The Forest People began to talk again in low voices and to point across the wilderness where a horseman came riding at full gallop toward the hills!

After a long time when no one seemed even to breathe, the horseman came close enough to be clearly seen. It was a warrior in full armor, with a red plume on his helmet. And there, behind him, sat Buzz! When the horse plunged over the last hill, and stood prancing, Buzz slid down to the ground, the warrior handed her something, and she ran to Heather.

Chief Elfstream and his archers, the children, Chief Goodshade, and everyone else watched as Buzz unwrapped a fold of soft doeskin and held out to Heather a beautiful shining belt-disk of bronze. "Wolf Stone sent this to you. He is now the chief." Buzz's voice trembled a little as she said, "He's coming for you, he's coming to take you away as soon as they bury his father."

Heather held the bronze disk in her hands. It glinted in the sunlight. She asked, "How did his father die?"

Buzz glanced as Goodshade, at Elfstream and his archers, and the children. Everyone stood very still, staring and listening. She spoke loudly so they could all hear. "Blue Wing was shooting at the girl warriors and one of his arrows killed Troll Tamer, and Great Elk died at the same time because there was a curse between him and Troll Tamer. When one of them died, the other one simply had to because anyway that is the way it was."

Buzz noticed the shock and fear in Goodshade's eyes and said, again quite loudly, "It was all an accident. Nobody blamed Blue Wing. They're sending him back home. I think he's in that wagon that drove into the long wood. It wasn't his fault."

She touched Heather's hand and whispered, "I'm going with you and Wolf Stone. When I grow up I'm going to marry Badger, even if he already has several wives. But don't you worry about Wolf Stone. *You* are to be his only wife. Badger told me so."

As Heather fastened the sun-disk on her belt, the

children trilled like insects with excitement. Buzz did not even look at them, or at silent, scowling Elfstream, as she followed Heather down the hill.

To all the silent people standing on the sandy hill a sun-disk was the emblem of a strange and evil god, a sort of demon alive with dangerous and destructive powers. Not one of them would touch such an object of gleaming bronze. But boldly, right before their eyes, Heather had fastened it on her belt!

Proudly, hurt by their silent disapproval, Heather walked across the open glade and into the forest. Buzz followed her. Neither of them looked back. When they were out of sight among the trees, Heather said, a little sadly, "Elfstream has made them all hate me."

"Is he bad?" whispered Buzz.

"No. But he makes everyone do just what he wants. Because he's so old, I guess. You watch, he'll try to make me give Wolf Stone's sun-disk to the tree."

"Don't you do it!"

"I won't." Heather sighed. It was a sigh of relief and release. "Tomorrow I'll be far away . . ."

They glanced back toward the hills and walked slowly on among the trees. Behind them there was only silence. And Heather thought how different the silence between people was from the silence of the forest. She listened to birds and insects and leaves stirring peacefully. Then she found herself listening intently for some other voice that was not there. "Buzz!" she whispered. "I don't hear the spring!"

Buzz listened. The spring was silent.

They ran on to the spring and stood gazing at it in dismay. Where the clear cool water had burst musically out of the stone was only a glistening dampness. Not one drop of water fell into the pool. On its smooth, shining surface they saw an upside-down world of leaves and sky. Hardly daring to breathe, they leaned over the still water and saw the reflection of their own startled faces. In the shadow of a bough the reflected world vanished, and the water was as clear as air. Deep, deep below, gilded with silt, lay many ancient flint axes which had been offered to the god of the spring.

Heather could not understand why the spring had died so suddenly. She touched the warm, gleaming bronze on her belt. Its magic could never have worked so quickly. She could see that no water had splashed into the pool for hours; and she had worn the disk for only a few minutes. If the crystal body of the god had died deep under the earth, that would be a dreadful thing for the people of Oakwood. They would have to move away and find new water. She refused to believe anything so terrible. No, the wind had drunk too deeply, that was all. The spring was only sleeping, waiting for the rains to waken it.

She wondered if her mother knew what had happened.

But of course Tree Woman would know. And Good-shade and Elfstream. She sighed. Now they would all try to make her give the sun-disk to the spring to bring it back to life. There were tears in her eyes, and fear, and defiance. How could her love for Wolf Stone have anything to do with it! This was one spring of many throughout the forest. It was not a god above all the world, like the sun! Still, gazing at the unruffled surface of the pool, she longed to hear its happy laughter again, and in her heart she prayed as she had since she was a child, "Make me as pure and clear as you are so I may speak the oldest words happily as you—as you once did."

Buzz too was thinking about the spring. She said nothing to Heather about her thoughts because she knew, she *knew* why the spring had died. Because she had taken from it a sacrificial stone ax, the one she had given to Eagle. Suddenly she burst into violent sobbing, and to Heather's amazement ran blindly away into the forest.

Tree Woman's voice spoke softly behind Heather. "Your father and Chief Elfstream want you to give the image of the sun to the spring."

Heather touched the precious bronze ornament. "It is Wolf Stone's promise that he will come for me. If I gave it to the spring, he would say I had given his god into the power of our gods. When he comes for me, if he tells me that I may, I will give it to the spring." The silence between Heather and her mother deepened.

Tree Woman went back to her house, and Heather stayed on by the still pool wondering why Buzz had acted so strangely. Suddenly she felt someone watching her. It was her father and old, white-bearded Elfstream. They watched her for a moment, and then went silently away.

ELFSTREAM and his archers had made camp in the meadow beyond the village. Goodshade stood alone in the windy glade waiting until a wagon came rattling and bouncing out of the long wood. With a flurry of dust sweeping before it, the wagon stopped, and out of it leaped a dozen rough, slit-eared slaves. They sprawled in the lee of a bush and rubbed the sand out of their eyes.

Eagle, with a leather sack in his hand, swaggered across to Goodshade. Pointing with his chin, he asked the tall, fair-haired man who watched him coldly, "Are you the chief of this village?"

Goodshade nodded, and asked, "Where is Blue Wing?"

Eagle shrugged. "When I left camp he was teaching Great Elk how to fight with bow and arrows." Squatting on his haunches, he dumped the contents of his sack on the ground. There were five bronze knives, a piece of amber, two bracelets, a short length of broken chain, and Great Elk's gold cup. "I want to buy the tree Blue Wing showed me. The tree with a tall curved bough." Then he added, "Not the one you think is a god."

Goodshade picked up the gold cup and examined it. He put it down and glanced over the other objects. He selected the two unmatched bracelets, one small link from the broken chain, and walked away toward the bee tree.

Eagle was puzzled by his choice, but satisfied. He stowed the more valuable things in his sack, shouted through the wind to his slaves to bring ropes and axes, and they followed Goodshade.

The slaves were soon climbing high in the tree, lopping off small branches as they climbed. Others chopped by turns at the base of its curved, unbranching bough. Soon they had cut a notch halfway through it at the base where it swept out from the massive trunk. They were skillful with their axes, but they had never worked in so tall a tree, never in such a wind. They grumbled and cursed Eagle for his confusing commands shouted up to them over the rattle of leaves. They dropped branches close to him, making him leap about and shout more wildly than ever.

Suddenly the wind fell, and the blows of axes sounded sharply in a heavy silence. Then, as suddenly, a twisting gust howled out of the sky and struck the tree. Its fibers groaned and where it had been deeply cut it snapped, creaking, crashing heavily into the surrounding forest, its base split, ruining it for use as the keel of a ship.

The tumbled slaves howled, and burrowed like rats in the tangle of twigs and leaves. Bruised and enraged, they heaved branches aside and emerged from the clutter of destruction. Out of one white, hollow branch came an angry drone as a swarm of bees attacked the slaves who ran away toward the glade, slapping themselves wildly.

Clenching and unclenching his big hands, Eagle looked up into a bright emptiness of windy sky. Near the edge of the forest, he found his sack where he had hidden it. When he reached the clearing, the wagon was already clattering away to the south, now visible, now shrouded in blowing sand. When it vanished over the hills, he turned and walked with loose, ambling indifference toward the north, still clutching Great Elk's gold cup in his sack.

Goodshade, who had watched this, returned to his village.

Beyond the rise where Wolf Stone's tent had stood,
two graves were dug. There, Troll Tamer and
Great Elk were buried side by side, the priest in his white
robe, the old chief wearing the amber breastplate over
his dented armor. Food was left beside both, a beaker
of water for the priest, ale for Great Elk, although not
in his own cup which could not be found. The lurs
lamented softly as rocks were piled on both graves.

Wolf Stone remained there alone after the service,
after everyone had gone back to continue as quietly as
possible the tasks of rolling skin tents into bales and
packing them on wagons, or herding the bawling cattle

ahead of the march to the south, of setting the great sun-disk on its six wheels and starting it on its way, led by priests, followed by warriors and slaves on foot. Wagons crowded with children and women followed.

Beside the lake, a troop of mounted warriors and Doves waited to escort the new chief.

Great Elk's tent was already packed in bales, all but the awning. In its shade sat Wolf Stone's counselors, two old men who had served Great Elk for years, and the captains. Beyond the awning the chief's wagon waited. There, unnoticed, hot and miserable in the sun, sat Blue Wing, his arms and legs tied to a wheel.

Wolf Stone stood beside his father's grave, listening to the voice of the wind. It seemed to tell him that Great Elk had stepped aboard the sun's ship and was now coursing the sky. "Now," sang the wind, "he has come to the sun's land. The woman he loves embraces him. He is no longer alone. She touches the amber on his breast . . ." For a moment Wolf Stone could almost see the far world where they stood. Then a soft radiance enfolded everything and the vision was gone. Only the voice of the wind remained. But he was at peace.

He returned to the littered and deserted camp. Seated in the wooden chair his father had prized, he took his place before the council. What he now intended to say was clear in his mind. He called each of his counselors by name, and each replied with a gesture of loyalty.

"It won't be easy," said Oxenstar, smiling, "to be led by a man younger than any of us. But I have already seen enough power shine out of this brother of ours to believe the god commands him."

One of the old men arose and addressed Wolf Stone. "We have been discussing certain changes it is said you intend to make in our ways. Do you intend to serve as our high priest as your father used to? Is that true?"

"It is true."

"Do you intend to change our morning and evening worship to only a few moments of song to the rising and setting sun, the dancing ceremony to occur only four times each year at the turn of the seasons? Is this your plan?"

"It is," said Wolf Stone.

The old man sat down, smiling and nodding to those about him. "That's how it was when I was a boy."

"I knew you would approve those changes," said the young chief. "But I am not sure you will like some others I have in mind." He gazed out past the lake and for a moment forgot what he had meant to say.

Oxenstar broke into his thoughts of Heather by asking, "Where will you lead us now?"

Wolf Stone replied slowly. "Do you remember where we lived as children? Do you remember when our father, who was young then, caught and tamed a herd of wild horses? Do you remember trapping fish in the lake, and snaring waterbirds for their feathers? Do you remember the elk that each year crossed that grassy land owned by no one?"

Badger said gruffly, "I have often wondered why we ever left that place."

"I will tell you why," said one of the old men. "Because when trading tribes stopped coming through there, Great Elk had no one to fight and rob. Ever since, he's dragged us about looking for trouble, and finding it."

Wolf Stone smiled. "At least he made men of his sons."

"And of our girls as well!" laughed Badger.

Oxenstar grumbled, "I say we take all swords and horses away from the Doves and teach them manners!"

Badger snorted, "If you took away their toys, they'd learn witchcraft and poison us! Simply let them take a husband without killing anyone! They never get over bragging about it. You should hear my wives!"

"That will be the first change in the ways of our young women," said Wolf Stone quietly. "They may take a husband without killing an enemy. They will no longer fight in battle. They will carry arms only when they dance in ceremonies."

Badger shouted happily. Oxenstar glanced toward the Doves beside the lake and said grimly, "Wait until I tell this to somebody I know!"

"This does not affect me," said Wolf Stone, "since I intend to take only one wife, a girl of the Forest People."

The captains pretended to be surprised. Badger nodded his head wisely. "I guessed all that scouting ahead wasn't simply to catch rabbits."

Wolf Stone smiled. He stood up and said, "We will now take Blue Wing back to his village. And I . . ." He glanced toward the wagon where Blue Wing had been tied. He reached for his sword.

In some way, Blue Wing had freed himself and was standing a little distance away toward the lake, a wild light of jealous fury in his eyes. Somewhere he had found an unbroken arrow. He had restrung his bow.

The Doves had been watching him, curious, and then startled as he fitted the arrow to the bowstring and aimed it at Wolf Stone. As the arrow flew, six whizzing swords pierced Blue Wing.

The arrow pinned Wolf Stone's right upper arm to his side. He sat down stiffly and carefully in his chair. His face went white as Badger drew the shaft out of his arm. "When the wound is bandaged," said the young chief briskly, "we will all ride to Oakwood."

His arm was bandaged, his horse led up, he stood, but sank down again, a sweat of pain on his face. "I think the stone point is still in my side."

While the point was dug out, Wolf Stone watched the sun sinking close to the western horizon, and clouds blazing gold and scarlet in the east. In his mind was an image of Heather; in his heart, pride and happiness and wonder because she loved him. He hardly felt the pain. But it tired him. To Oxenstar he said wearily, "Go to Heather and tell her I will come for her after I have slept."

Oxenstar and Badger sat beside him as he slept. They were disturbed by his troubled breathing. They knew nothing of healing herbs and could only hold his fevered hand and wipe the dew of sweat from his closed eyes.

"I think he is more deeply hurt than we know," whispered Badger.

Oxenstar turned away to hide his unmanly tears. "If he dies . . ."

"If he dies," said Badger gruffly, "I will never again dance to a god so false!"

"Nor will I," said Oxenstar.

Clouds filled the eastern sky, blue where they loomed out of the sea, white as shell where sunlight still touched them. Heat lightning flickered without sound, and the clouds glowed like embers under ashes. The wind had died away. Not a leaf stirred. From far away came a rumble of thunder.

Goodshade sat outside his house, gazing toward the hills.

Heather came out and sat beside him. Often in the evening they sat there together, talking a little, like old friends, about anything at all. Tonight Goodshade said nothing. Nor did she, for a while. They were both aware of the bronze disk on her belt. When at last she spoke it was abruptly. "It wasn't Blue Wing's fault." Goodshade was silent. His silence said that when she went away with the Sun People he would never think of her again. Her lips trembled. She felt the sadness that surged through his heart. "I don't believe Blue Wing taught the Sun People anything dangerous." Still Goodshade was silent. She stood up and looked around the village. "I wonder where Buzz is." She walked over to a tree and touched its rough bark as if she would never see a tree again. She picked a frond of fern and a blossom of milfoil and stuck them in her blouse. "I think I will try to find Buzz," she said. Her mother was in the cooking shelter mixing marsh-myrtle leaves and crushed cranberries with the last of the honey. It was almost dark, but no stars showed. "Have you seen Buzz?" asked Heather.

"No," said Tree Woman.

Reindeer started to come out of the house with a jar full of water. Her eyes caught the glint of the sun-disk on Heather's belt. Quickly she went back inside.

Heather glanced at Littleman who was sitting against his wall. She went over to ask if he had seen Buzz. Before she got there he had gone inside and dropped the painted hide over his door.

She walked aimlessly across the meadow, thinking about old Fang and his puppies. And about the Swampwife. And the bee tree that lay broken in the forest. She went to the camp of Elfstream's archers, but they were too intent upon some game played with painted sticks to notice her. For the third time that evening she went up the mound and peeked into the empty cave under the stones.

Darkness had deepened. Lightning flickered in the windless sky. She went to the glade and on among the trees. Not an insect was chirping, not even a sleepy bird. She looked at the broken tangle of the bee tree and into the open sky above it. A flash of lightning flushed the moss and leaves a vivid green. She held her breath until thunder shook the stillness.

Then she heard, almost as far away as the thunder, a sound of horse's hoofs. It could only be Wolf Stone coming for her!

She ran back to the village. The horseman was already there, dismounting, walking toward Goodshade. It was not Wolf Stone.

A wind along the ground flapped the wolf pelts that covered the doorways. In the gray light, the small wooden houses looked as old as the trees themselves.

Goodshade walked toward Oxenstar, who waited to speak until Heather came up and stood beside her father. Then, gruffly, the young chief of the Sun People said, "Blue Wing was killed because he killed Wolf Stone with an arrow."

There was nothing more to say. Blue Wing and Wolf Stone were both dead.

Oxenstar walked stiffly to his horse and rode away. Goodshade walked back to his house. Tree Woman stood in the doorway. He stepped past her and went inside.

Heather walked slowly over to her mother and unfastened the sun-disk from her belt. "For the tree or the spring as you wish," she murmured. She gave the disk to Tree Woman and went through the darkness to the mound and up its slope to the great boulders. She climbed to the capstone and sat there until lightning began to flash over the forest. One massive, rumbling peal of thunder rolled away, and a wind sighed, a cool wind smelling of rain. When the first big drops splashed down, Heather crept into the dark little cave under the stones.

When the storm broke, she heard the crashing of thunder and the splashing of rain only as a muted rumbling and rustling far away from the warm, dry darkness of the cave. But she knew that the heart of the sky had burst. Violet and green flashes lit up the veils of rain, and now and then a dull smoky red tinged the darkness as a tree was struck and blazed up. Once, after a crackling roar of thunder, a brighter glow lit up the clouds. The Swampwife's hut had been struck and was burning. At last the clouds smoldered to ashes, and the storm moved on. Thunder sounded farther and farther away, and then was silent. Outside the cave, drops pattered and spattered, until they simply dripped, fewer and fewer, like small tinkling bells, and Heather fell asleep.

When she awoke, the sun was shining. Not only one sun, but many small suns, glinting and glistening in the jewels of water drops that fringed the stone entrance to the cave. As she crept out into the morning light, the drops fell sparkling about her, touching her arms and face, making her shiver. She smelled the rain-washed air and heard birds singing as they flew across the sky. It seemed as if the world had forgotten the storm and the darkness, as if it had wept all sorrow away.

She had not forgotten the storm. But this sunny, golden morning was more real, as real as the dream she had just awakened from. In her dream, Wolf Stone came riding down into the glade. Bees were humming among the flowers as he sat there on his horse in his golden-bronze armor, waiting for her. She knew it was a dream. But it seemed as real as the morning world she ran lightly down to meet.

In his small field, Goodshade was digging with his hoe to drain the flooded water away from his wheat. When she came through the zigzag gate, he paused and smiled, a smile warm with love.

From somewhere in the forest Heather heard axes cutting wood, and stone chipping stone. These were good sounds, the sounds of building a lonely peace she could not quite understand.

Tree Woman had seen Heather run down the mound, and now came into the field, barely able to squeeze in through the zigzag gate. She held Heather in her arms as if she were still a child. There was no shadow or silence between them. After glancing at Goodshade, who nodded and returned to his work, Tree Woman said gently, "Buzz is gone. Last night she died in the storm. Lightning struck the Swampwife's hut where she was sleeping. Elfstream's men are carving a coffin for her small burnt bones."

Heather went across the glade—the glade where Wolf Stone waited for her in her dream—and on, out to the broken bee tree. The litter of leaves and branches had been cleared away, built into a new hedge around a new field. Elfstream's men were busy with flint axes and knives. They had cut and were carving two halves of the great split oak bough. It seemed a very large coffin for so small a child as Buzz.

Heather went deeper into the forest where the voices of the earth had spoken to her. She held her breath and listened. The voices still spoke to her, even more clearly than before. And beyond these she heard another sound —the chipping of stone on stone. She went toward this sound. A sound that was mostly silence.

The rain had not awakened the spring. It still slept. It was still only a tinge of mossy dampness on the rock. On the hill above it, Elfstream's men had dug widely and deeply. In the moist hollow between mounds of earth and rock they had spread a floor of small stones. They had completed their work and gone away.

Heather could not understand what they had been doing. Perhaps it was some way to bring life back to the spring.

The ancient way would be to offer a sacrifice of something treasured. Something . . . or someone!

Her heart beat heavily as she heard a sound of chanting. Out of the forest and slowly up the path Goodshade and Tree Woman came marching, past the pool and the sleeping spring. They were dressed in ceremonial robes. Behind them, wearing the skin of a red deer, with deer antlers on his head, came bearded Elfstream, chief of all the forest chieftains. After him came the people of the village. And the archers, bearing on their shoulders the oaken coffin that was much too large for little Buzz.

At last Heather understood as out of the forest flitted the Shadow Dancers, their faces and bodies smeared with white clay. As they danced about her, rattles of seed pods on their wrists and ankles rustled like rain.

With trembling hands, Goodshade tied the sun-disk to Heather's belt. Tree Woman danced up to her with ceremonial small steps and held out to her a small birch-bark bucket. In it was a cool summer drink that smelled faintly of clover.

Heather felt a dark wind swooping down out of the

sky. She shivered, and closed her eyes. In a moment her fear was gone, swept away by the sunny stillness of the forest, the timeless voice of peace. She opened her eyes and smiled as she thought of Wolf Stone waiting for her in the glade only a little distance away. She drank deeply.